Collision

OF THE

Heart

Collision
OF THE Heart

LAURIE ALICE EAKES

Waterfall
PRESS

Published by Waterfall Press

www.brilliancepublishing.com

Amazon, the Amazon logo, and Waterfall Press are trademarks of Amazon.com, Inc., or its affiliates.

ISBN-13: 9781503936287
ISBN-10: 1503936287

Cover design by Mike Heath

Printed in the United States of America

To the people of my home state. My fondest childhood memories are set in winter, as Michiganders know what to do with snow: have fun.

AUTHOR'S NOTE

Several years ago, this book was published under the title *The Professor's Heart* during the brief period in which Harlequin Love Inspired owned the rights to the Heartsong line of romances. Because it was for book clubs only, relatively few people knew of the line or the book's existence. Since I love this second-chance-at-love romance set in my native state of Michigan during the winter, I am thrilled to have this second chance to share this story with you.

Chapter One

Hillsdale, Michigan
February 8, 1856
Midnight

In ten minutes, the westbound train would reach the town Euphemia Roper once vowed to never set foot in again.

Hillsdale, Michigan, was the town Euphemia—Mia to her friends—had called home longer than anywhere else in her twenty-six years and the town she had left with a broken heart. Only opportunity knocking too loudly to be ignored had drawn her back. For a week, she would research the story that would establish her as a professional lady of letters, while she avoided encounters with Ayden Benaiah Goswell.

She twisted in her train seat and rubbed frost from a patch of glass with her gloved fingers. The action accomplished little beyond making her hand damp through the knitted wool. The lights of Osseo had already dimmed beyond a veil of falling snow. The train gathered speed.

So did Euphemia's heart.

Muscles twitching in her legs, Euphemia tucked her handbag under one arm and her writing portfolio under the other. Rustling pages, snapping locks, and a child asking if they were there yet rose like a wave before a high wind. Euphemia rose to get up the aisle and near the door before the train stopped so she could be one of the first passengers to disembark. Others preceded her, including a child barely old enough to walk. He paused to grasp the side of her seat.

"Are you lost?" Euphemia leaned toward the boy. Someone should be frantically searching for the little one.

"Nana?" His quivering lower lip protruded.

"Uh-oh. Don't cry. I'll find your mo—"

The train whistle blasted its mournful call into the night. Several women exclaimed. Mia jumped, and the child let out a howl loud enough to wake any passenger still asleep after the whistle blast.

"You poor baby." Euphemia set her handbag and portfolio on her empty seat and crouched before the boy, her skirt billowing around her. "I'll find your momma." She raised her voice. "Is anyone here missing a—"

With the cacophony of a hundred metal sheets slamming together, the train shuddered to a halt. The car floor bucked. The baby, Euphemia, and luggage tumbled across the aisle. Passengers screamed.

"We've wrecked!" someone shouted.

The car rocked on its wheels. More cases fell. More passengers shrieked.

"We're going to derail!"

"We're going to die!"

"Fire! Fire!"

No more than the usual tendrils of coal smoke filled the car, but passengers stampeded for the door. One wrist throbbing, Euphemia snatched up the child and dove back into her seat. The contents of her handbag crunched under her feet. Her writing case remained on the seat.

"Help me!" A woman's cries rose above the hubbub of wailing, shouting, shoving passengers. "My leg. I can't walk! I can't move."

"Stay here." Euphemia laid the child on the seat. She picked up her writing case before she headed for the back of the car, toward the crying woman.

"Where are you?" Euphemia called.

Banging, wailing, and bellowing drowned out the woman's reply—if the woman replied. She could have fainted—or worse.

Euphemia's heart leaped into her throat, pulsing hard enough to choke her. She paused to take a deep, steadying breath. Calm would accomplish more than panic. Enough chaos reigned behind her. She didn't need to add to it.

She took a step toward where she thought she heard the woman crying for help. The car tilted. A piece of luggage slammed into her legs. She grabbed for a seatback to steady herself, and pain blazed through her left wrist. She tucked her writing case beneath her left forearm in order to free her right hand. It was all right, strong, capable of groping in the near total darkness between the seats for the woman who had been sobbing and calling for help or for anyone else unable to ask for assistance. Three seats lay between Euphemia and the end of the railroad car. She checked on, between, and under each one.

"Ma'am?" Euphemia shouted above the ruckus of what seemed like more people than the car—or the entire train—could have carried. "Are you there?"

Behind her, a baby wailed. The one she'd found or someone else's. *Must get back to him, find his momma or nurse. First, the woman.*

She reached the last row. Her questing fingers touched a shoulder between the seats and wedged against the rear exit.

A hand clasped hers. "You've got to help me."

"I'll do what I can." Euphemia stooped to get her arm under the woman. "Can you lean on me?"

"I think my leg is broke." The hand gripped Euphemia's nearly hard enough to break bones. "I can't walk. I need to get out of here."

"We all do." Euphemia freed her hand.

"Don't leave me."

"I must go to get help." Euphemia took a step back, turned, and headed up the aisle, calling, "Any men here? There's a woman here who needs to be carried."

No response from inside the car. Outside, a few lights bobbed, perhaps a promise of rescue on its way.

She paused at her seat. The toddler still lay there. He no longer sobbed or so much as whimpered. Surely, such quietness wasn't normal for a child.

"Anyone missing a baby?" She grimaced at how ridiculous the words sounded when shouted.

If a woman had mislaid her child, she would be doing the asking. Yet no cries of a frantic mother—or anyone else seeking a little boy—rose above the ruckus. That made two people to help, the woman and the baby

Euphemia patted the toddler. "I'll be right back."

She started up the aisle. "I need someone to carry a woman. Please."

Someone grabbed her arm. "Can you help me, young lady?" The voice shook. The hand shook.

"Of course. Hold on to my arm." Euphemia continued toward the exit.

"Can someone help me with these children?" A woman yelled, her voice breaking.

"I can't find my cane." The voice cracked from the throat of a man who sounded ancient.

"I'll return to help you shortly," Euphemia assured the supplicants.

She must get her current charge off the train, aid those she could, find assistance for those she couldn't. She must work fast. Too much smoke filled the air now, and that stench of hot metal twisted her insides like one of those new pretzel rolls. Judging from the smell, the train was on fire.

"I said it would burn!" The voice rose to a shriek. "Out. We have to get out of here!"

Passengers began to push and shove. The hubbub grew deafening, no voice loud enough to rise above another.

"Quiet, all of you." Deep and authoritative, a man's voice penetrated the chaos. "We will get you off one at a time and faster if you stay calm."

Euphemia's knees buckled. Breath snagged in her throat. Spots danced before her eyes.

She knew that voice. Not so long ago, her ears strained to hear it calling her name, murmuring he loved her. Now the last thing she wanted was to push forward with the rest of the passengers and meet him face-to-face.

She freed her arm from the older woman's hold and tapped the shoulder of a man in front of her. "Will you please help this lady? I need to assist others."

If the man said anything, the noise inside the car drowned out his words, but he reached a hand behind him. Euphemia placed the elderly woman's fingers in his and then slipped past her to the woman with the children.

"Stay here for a few more minutes," she said. "It's too crowded up there right now."

"But the train's on fire!" The woman sobbed as loudly as her offspring. "We'll burn alive."

"No, no. The fire is a long way off." Euphemia smiled to make her assurance more convincing.

She did speak the truth. A dozen cars lay between the engine boiler and theirs. With the wetness of snow, the fire shouldn't spread quickly. Wind might carry sparks, though, and then . . .

She tugged a woolly cap more snuggly around the younger child's ears. "I'll be back in a minute to help get your children up to the door. There . . . there's a man there, helping people down."

She swung away. Pulling on this boy's cap reminded her of the toddler. She must look to his safety. The woman with the broken leg still needed aid.

The old man caught hold of her coat sleeve. "My cane. I can't find my cane. You said you'd help me find my cane."

"I did, yes." Her movements awkward with her left forearm pressing her writing case to her chest, Euphemia sank to her knees and began to grope around on the floor for the cane. She found it amid a pile of small parcels wedged beneath a seat across the aisle, yanked it free, and handed it to the gentleman. "Will you be all right from here? I have a baby to look after and a woman with a broken leg."

She didn't wait for the man to answer. The toddler had begun to wail. She reached him and started to lift him. Her toe struck something on the floor, and she remembered her spilled handbag. She must gather what she could of her possessions, her purse at the least. She needed money to pay for her lodging at the boardinghouse and meals. She needed her return train ticket.

She settled for patting his back. "I'm here, baby. We'll find your mother. She's got to be here somewhere. Or someone had you with them."

Once again, she felt around on the dirty and rather wet floor, gathering up what objects she encountered and shoving them into her handbag. If they proved not to be hers, she would seek to locate the owners later.

"All right, then." She shoved a bottle of scent, miraculously unbroken, into the bag. "Off to find your momma."

"Nana." The baby snuffled.

"Nana." Euphemia tried to lift the boy. She couldn't do it with one arm, but she couldn't leave her writing case.

She set it down and picked up the toddler. Her left wrist protested. Hissing a gasp of pain through her teeth, she gathered her case and headed for the front of the car, calling over her shoulder, "I'm going for help now, ma'am."

No one answered. That wasn't a good sign. The woman must have lost consciousness, which meant she was seriously hurt.

Euphemia quickened her steps. In front of her, the crowd surged forward.

"One at a time." Ayden's voice boomed above the other voices, more like a preacher's than a professor's, as full and rich as summer cream.

Euphemia shut her eyes. If only her ears could close, she could pretend he wasn't there, not a dozen feet away, their encounter inevitable.

"Just jump, ma'am. I'll catch you, and if I don't, the snow's as soft as a featherbed." He laughed as though this were some new game.

His light tone worked. The passengers calmed. They stopped shoving one another and lined up for their turns like obedient schoolchildren. Consequently, the line moved more quickly. Four seats, three seats, then only two seats were between Euphemia and the doorway. With each step, her stomach knotted more tightly. Her heart beat as though threatening to pound its way out of her ribs. She should have prayed to avoid Ayden. She should have dyed her hair and pretended to be someone else. She should have—

"Next?" Ayden directed.

Euphemia opened her eyes. She was next, or rather, the child was next.

She hastened to the doorway. "Take this child. I'll return." She spoke in breathless accents.

"You need to stay with your child, ma'am," Ayden said.

He didn't recognize her—yet.

She leaned down. "Take him. He's heavy."

"Ma'am, you can't—"

Squirming now, the toddler slipped from Euphemia's one-armed hold. Ayden caught him and shot an annoyed glance Euphemia's way.

Light from a lantern hanging from the side of the car shone on his face, etching every strong, chiseled bone like a sculptor's tool. A knitted hat covered most of his thick, dark hair. His deep-blue eyes widened. His mouth gaped.

"Mia?" He barely whispered his pet name for her.

"Mia, *mi amore*" was what he had dubbed her throughout their courtship.

A lump rose in her throat. The lantern light blurred, and she spun on her heel. "Others. I need help with others. There's a woman in here with a broken leg."

"Whose baby is this?" he shouted after her.

"I don't know." She choked on the tightness in her throat.

"Mia."

The baby's wails drowned out anything else he might have said to her. The crying grew fainter. He must be moving away from the train. Good. She could help the woman with the children. But she couldn't help the woman with the injured leg on her own.

She reached the mother and took the hand of one of the children. "I can help you outside now."

She led the child to the doorway. "Stay there. I'll lift you down."

She glanced at the ground. Without steps or platform, the floor of the car looked half a story high. Without assistance, she was going to fall flat on her face.

"Mia, wait." Ayden sprinted across the snow-laden ground as though it were flat, dry pavement. "I'll catch you."

She'd rather fall flat on her face or stay in the train than have him anywhere near her, but to her right, the front of the train blazed like a bonfire. Heat reached back on every gust of wind.

She jumped.

Ayden caught her around the waist and held her suspended above the snow. "You're too thin."

"And you're rude. Now set me down." She pushed at his chest with her portfolio.

He set her down. "Straight ahead. Pa's just arrived with the sleigh. We'll take these people home."

"I thought you might."

"You can come, too, you know."

She shook her head. "Not a good idea. I'm staying at the boardinghouse."

"I expect it's already full." He moved past her to lift down the children and their mother.

Euphemia didn't move. "I have a reservation."

"Did you intend to stop here, ma'am?" Ayden asked the mother.

"We were going to my parents in Chicago." She sobbed as hard as her two children. "I don't know nobody here."

"That's all right. You can stay with us. Mia, will you take one of the children and show this lady to our sleigh? It's about a hundred feet straight ahead, with the two lamps on it." He started toward another car.

"Wait," Euphemia called. "There's another woman in there. She's injured. She says she can't walk."

"I'll get her." Ayden hoisted himself inside the car.

Euphemia gave the mother and her children a reassuring smile. "I'll help you all get through this snow to the Goswell sleigh. You'll be safe there."

"I don't know, ma'am." The woman clutched her children to her skirts. "They're strangers."

"You can trust them." She grimaced. "Not that you have any reason to trust me."

Somehow, that remark seemed to reassure the woman. She released her hold on the taller of the two children, a girl inadequately clothed for the weather. "Can you help her? I never seen such snow."

"I have. It's like walking through a bag of flour," Euphemia said.

"Cold flour," the girl added through her snuffles.

Euphemia took her hand. "Really cold flour. I hope you can walk. You're too grown up for me to carry you."

"I'm seven."

"Really grown up." Euphemia clutched the child's mittened fingers and started toward the twin carriage lamps suspended from a sleigh, no doubt the one she had taken dozens of rides in over the years, tucked up between Ayden and his younger sister or his mother or cuddled just with him . . .

She slammed the door on those memories and trudged forward. Newly fallen, the snow lay in fluffy drifts atop a layer of hard-packed snow from another storm. She sank up to her knees in places. The child struggled beside her. Her mother carried the boy. Each step proved an effort. There was no way Euphemia could walk into town. But surely someone would give her a ride, someone other than the Goswells.

Except she couldn't go into town yet. She must get these children and their mother to the Goswell sleigh. She had to find that toddler's people. Once she accomplished those tasks, she could find transportation into Hillsdale.

Plan made, she continued to tramp through the snow. Her feet felt like the packed-down stuff, heavy, solid, immovable. She didn't want to see Mr. Goswell any more than she wanted to see Ayden again. He had been a father to her, more so than her own parent, who had disappeared in pursuit of nameless dreams only to return when those dreams faded or grew dull, until he disappeared permanently. Her father's last words to her had been "I'll be back." Mr. Goswell's last words had been "I'm so disappointed in the two of you that it hurts."

Her response was nothing she was proud to recall, and a fresh wave of guilt stabbed her as he loomed before her. Unlike Ayden's hair, Mr. Goswell's hair was gray rather than mahogany brown, but his eyes were still as blue and his smile as warm as his son's. "Euphemia Roper, what a sight for sore eyes. I knew you'd be back."

"I'm not returning. This is a brief stop for business purposes." She
kept her tone neutral. "Right now, Ayden sent me over with this family."

Mr. Goswell squeezed her shoulder. "Good. You'll stay with us."

"No, I—"

"I have that little one tucked up until we find his people. And
whom do we have here?"

"Some passengers who don't have a place to stay in Hillsdale."

"Yes, they do—with us." Mr. Goswell crouched to be eye-to-eye
with the children. "Would you like to come to our house for soup and
biscuits?"

The children stood in silence, turning into little snowmen beneath
the tumbling flakes.

"I . . . I don't have much money," the mother protested.

"They won't want money." Euphemia touched the woman's arm.
"I know the Goswells. They have lots of room and will feed you until
you cry for mercy."

Kind, generous, godly—all words to describe the Goswell family. She should want to stay with them. She shouldn't have left them
behind. She hadn't wanted to leave them behind, not permanently. She
and Ayden were supposed to return to Hillsdale for holidays, but Ayden
chose to stay instead of choosing to love her.

She shook off the hurt like snow accumulating on her coat and
held out her hand to draw the woman forward. "Is Mrs. Goswell in the
kitchen already?"

"The minute we heard the wreck." Mr. Goswell returned his attention to the children. "Would you like a sleigh ride?"

The children nodded. Their mother made protesting noises in her
throat.

Mr. Goswell glanced up at Euphemia. "Will, uh, you stay to help
me with these little ones?"

"I need to look for the baby's mother or whoever should have been
in charge of him." Euphemia stepped back. Her foot sank into a pile of

soft snow, and the crystallized wetness tumbled over the top of her boot to soak her stocking and freeze her foot. "Perhaps this lady can help."

Mr. Goswell rested his hand on Euphemia's shoulder. "She already has her own two, and you shouldn't be charging off on your own through this crowd at night. It's not safe."

"I've been in worse," Euphemia said.

"I'm happy to see to the little one to pay my way," the woman said.

"There's no need," Mr. Goswell began.

"That's an excellent idea." Euphemia recognized the woman's need to contribute to spare her pride. "If you go to the Goswells' house, I'll know where to find you when I find the baby's people." Without further ado, she yanked her foot from the snowdrift and headed toward the train, the worst of the crowd and the blazing fire creeping back from the engine.

"I'll be back to fetch you," Mr. Goswell shouted after her, but she continued without glancing behind her.

The going grew rougher with each step. Snow clung to her skirt and petticoats, weighing them down. More snow filled her boots. She should have gone into town with Mr. Goswell. His wife would have all the fires going and hot coffee on the stove. But duty called.

Euphemia approached a group of women huddled together. "Are any of you missing a child about a year and a half old?"

The women stared at her, their faces blank with shock in the flickering light of the burning train.

"No," one finally answered.

"If you hear of anyone, send them to the Goswell house." Euphemia turned away.

She went around, asking another group and then another. The answer remained the same—no one had heard of anyone seeking a baby like the one she described. Plenty of people sought loved ones. They wandered through the snow and stench of burning coal like sheep without their shepherd despite the dozens of townspeople who moved through them, talking, soothing, gathering the stranded passengers to transport them into town. Every conversation focused on the train—or more specifically, the *trains*. Off their schedules, the eastbound and westbound locomotives had crashed.

"The eastbound didn't have no headlight," one man said again and again. "It didn't have no headlight."

Frozen to her bones, Euphemia paused on snow packed as hard as ice from scores of feet and the heat of the fire. Mere yards away, the trains blazed, some of their cars broken free of their couplings and toppled over. Others leaned at a precarious angle, and the cars farther back, like the one she'd ridden in, appeared undamaged.

"What a mess." She took in each detail, committing it to memory.

If only she owned a camera and knew how to take photographs, this incident would do more for her journalism career at *Ladies' Monthly Fashion* than any of the stories she wrote. She should take notes, write down snatches of conversations. The conflagration provided enough light for her to see a page in her portfolio.

Careful of her throbbing wrist, she opened her writing case and extracted a pencil and paper. *Stray toddler. Woman broken leg. Old woman . . .*

"What are you doing?" Ayden snatched the pencil from her gloved fingers.

"I'm taking notes so I don't forget any of my impressions." She held out her hand. "Please give me back my pencil."

He did so. "You always were taking notes on something." He smiled. A dimple flashed in his left cheek, and her heart performed a somersault inside her ribs.

No, no, no. She would not succumb to the charm of that smile, that boyish dent in his cheek, his deep, resonant voice.

She took a step away from him. "I should get into town, I suppose. I heard something about the churches opening up to help stranded passengers. Perhaps I can find that boy's people there. Did you get that woman help? I suppose Dr. Clark is run off his feet help—"

"Hush." Ayden laid a gloved finger across her lips. "You don't need to be nervous around me, Mia."

She laughed. "Why would you think I'm nervous around you?"

"Because you're talking too much." His smile faded. "And to answer your question, no, I did not help that woman. She wasn't there. The car was empty of people."

Chapter Two

Mia's eyes widened, dark against her face, which was washed of color in the lantern light and snow reflection. Ayden gazed into those green eyes, and his heart performed an acrobatic flip inside his chest. It was perhaps the tenth or so flip his heart had performed since he looked up at the doorway of the railroad carriage and saw her, the woman he had adored for nearly eight years now, returned to the town he loved.

She came home! his heart had cried.

Even if she had returned to stay in Hillsdale, he did not—would not—love her now, whatever his heart believed. Loving Mia Roper brought too much pain into his life. Charmaine Finney, daughter of the director of the Hillsdale College Classics Department, who was Ayden's superior, was the lady in his life. She, not Euphemia Roper, held the key to his future happiness.

Yet he could not forget how Mia had turned him inside out from the day he had met her and kept him off balance until the day she'd dealt him the blow that toppled his world. He'd rebuilt that world over the past year and a half. One look into her heart-shaped face, framed in some kind of white fur on her hood, should not send him reeling like a man struck on the head. He intended to marry Charmaine Finney, not let Mia tie him into knots again.

He turned his face to the cold blast of wind. "Let's get into town. Perhaps we can find that baby's people there."

The sooner he got her into town, the sooner he could forget about his misbehaving heart.

"There's no room on the sleigh."

"I have a horse."

She flashed a glare from beneath her lashes. "You expect me to ride with you?"

"It won't be the first time."

The reminder was a mistake. Too late, the words spilled out, evoking happier times of summer picnics and winter sledding parties.

She swung away. "I'll walk."

"Don't be a fool, Mia." He slipped his hand beneath her elbow and guided her toward the edge of the thinning crowd along the length of the wrecked westbound train. "You can ride behind me."

She would still have to hold on to him somehow, but not as closely as she would if she rode in front of him.

"It's less than ten minutes," he reminded her.

She said nothing, and simply slogged through the snow with her head bent against the wind. She bent her left arm, hugging that writing case of hers as if it were an infant, except her hand didn't touch it. Her fingers stood straight out inside the glove, as though they had frozen stiff in that position.

"Mia?" he asked as they tramped through the snow to his mount. "Is your hand all right?"

"My hand is perfectly all right, thank you." Her tone sounded as stiff as her fingers looked.

"Then let me have it so I can help you mount."

She pressed the writing case more tightly against her front. "I can mount once you're up."

"That would be interesting to watch if I were attending a farce. But since this is reality, I'm lifting you up."

She took a step back.

Ayden sighed. "How old are you now? Twenty-six?"

"January first, yes. Why?"

"I thought perhaps you'd have outgrown that stubbornness by now."

The corners of her mouth twitched upward. "It might be worse."

"It's nothing to be proud of."

He sounded like a curmudgeon, as he always did when speaking to his nineteen-year-old sister, Rosalie. A year and a half of persuading students to pay attention to his lectures must have aged him beyond his twenty-eight years.

"Mia, what are you afraid of?" he asked in a gentler voice.

"I'm not afraid of anything, Ayden Goswell. I would simply rather not spend more time with you than necessary."

"This falls under the necessary category."

No longer giving her a chance to protest, he picked her up by her waist, a waist that felt too slender through her thick coat and all the other things ladies wore, and hoisted her onto the back of his chestnut gelding. She never released her hold on that writing case or her handbag. The latter smacked him in the face. The horse, old, a little overweight, and steady, remained motionless through the ordeal of Mia arranging her skirts and then Ayden mounting.

"Hold on," he directed.

A tug on his coat told him she held the fabric and no more. He set the mount to a slow, even pace to accommodate the extra person perched behind him. All the way past stragglers finding their way toward Hillsdale, past the mail cars flaming with their paper contents, Ayden tried not to think about the lady perched behind him. He shoved memories away. He conjured images of Charmaine with her sunshine-yellow hair and big blue eyes. She was as sweet tempered as Mia was stubborn.

Charmaine did not cradle a writing case against her like it was a newborn or a shield, as Mia did. The portfolio's presence was a constant reminder of why he and Mia had broken their engagement. With every jolt of the horse's hooves on the uneven and snow-laden ground, a corner of the case jabbed Ayden's shoulder blade, interrupting his attempts to focus on thoughts of Charmaine, a jab to his pride, a stab to his heart.

He tried to shake off the wrong thoughts penetrating his head like the cold through his coat. "Shall I leave you at First Church?" His voice rang harsh in the quiet land between the wrecked trains and the town.

"Th-that would be b-best." She spoke through teeth clattering together loudly enough for Ayden to hear.

"Are you cold?"

Stupid question. Of course she was cold. Snow had begun to fall more heavily, and the stuff coated her, crusting on her skirt from knees to hem.

"Perhaps I should take you to the boardinghouse first," he suggested. "They'll have a fire, and you can change into something dry."

"I have nothing to change into. My luggage is back on that train."

Along with a host of other people's belongings, the fire would soon destroy her personal effects if it wasn't stopped. With the cold and snow, Ayden saw no way for the fire wagons to reach the conflagration.

"I'm not your c-concern, Ayden. I haven't been since you d-decided to stay here instead of going to Boston with me." Even through her cold-induced stammer, the acid dripped from her voice hot enough to melt the snow around them.

Ayden flinched. He jerked the reins, and the gelding halted.

In an instant, Mia slid to the ground. "There's a wagon ahead. I'll see if they'll give me a lift to Howell Street."

"Mia, don't." Ayden leaned down to rest his hand on her arm.

She drew her breath in through her teeth and jerked away from him.

Ayden leaped from the horse and grasped her shoulders. "What's wrong?"

"Nothing, I'm sure. Just a bit of a sprain."

Ayden took her left hand in his. "You said your hand was all right."

"It's my wrist. I fell when the trains collided."

He ground his teeth. "Splitting hairs, Mia, mi—" No, she wasn't his love any longer, though the idea that she had stayed to help so many people despite an injured arm reminded him of one of the many reasons why she had been his love. She was strong and courageous, caring and generous.

"I didn't want you to fuss," Mia said. "And you can't do anything about it here in the snow."

"I'll get you to Dr. Clark before I do anything else."

"I must find that baby's people."

"And what if your wrist is broken, not just sprained?"

"Oh, well, um . . ." She gulped. "All right, but let me walk. It's not far now, and I might be warmer moving."

"At least let me hold your portfolio."

She ignored his request and started along the ruts the wagon had left in its wake. Snow was beginning to fill them, but it was light and fluffy, easy to walk over. It silenced their footfalls and the gelding's hooves. Ahead of them, light from houses and businesses reflected off the whiteness to make the world glow. The wind carried the scent of wood smoke with its promise of warm fires, hot soup, and hotter coffee.

Ayden lengthened his stride and then slowed again so he remained at Mia's side. "Will you be all right if I leave you at Dr. Clark's?"

"Yes, of course." She walked with her head bent and both arms around her writing case.

"I'll help you find that child's people," Ayden offered.

"I'd rather you didn't."

So she didn't have to see him. Although she didn't say so, the certainty of the meaning behind her refusal of his help rang loud and clear through the night. And it stung like the pellets of white crystals against his face.

"It's been eighteen months, Mia," he burst out. "Surely after that much time you can forgive me."

"Yes, I can—forgive and forget. Or did you think I came back here to see you?"

"I wouldn't be so foolish. But you must have known you were likely to see me here."

"I expected to be able to get away from you if I did." She picked up her snow-crusted skirts in her good hand and increased her speed.

Ayden let her walk ahead of him. She had always carried too much pride on her shoulders. Far be it from him to remove it. He had dealt it too much damage the summer she left town.

With Mia walking a yard in front of Ayden, they finished the last half mile into town. The closer they drew to Hillsdale, the brighter the lights shone. Nearly every house and business glowed with candles, oil lamps, or lanterns in windows and hanging outside. Though a block off Howell, one of the main streets, First Church stood out the brightest and loudest. Ayden and Mia turned toward the building and began to wend their way through the wagons and sleighs lining the thorough-fare in front of the white building. Bedraggled, snow-covered people swarmed in and out of the front door, many crying, raging against the railroad's incompetence, and others pleading for help.

Dr. Clark's house and office lay farther on, but as Ayden and Mia began to pass the church, the doctor himself appeared in the door-way for a moment, engaged in conversation with one of his students, Miss Liberty Judd. She was dressed in a fancy green gown, and jewels sparkled in her hair, of all the ridiculous things.

Ayden closed the distance between Mia and himself. "You may as well stop here." He reached out his hand but didn't touch so much as her coat sleeve. "If you need anything while you're here, don't hesitate to come ask us. You know we'll do anything for you."

Except for the one thing she had asked of him.

He winced inside as he smiled outside.

"Thank you." She flashed him her quick, brilliant smile and swung toward the church.

Dr. Clark and Liberty would take care of Mia, attend to her injured wrist, get her to her room for the night, and get her anything else she needed. He must get home and help his parents and sister with the woman and three children they had gathered from the wreck.

He led his horse to the stable behind their back garden and rubbed him down. Stroking the gelding's chestnut mane reminded Ayden he had purchased that particular horse because the color matched Mia's shining hair. In spite of that illogical reason for buying a mount, the gelding had proven to be a fine animal, placid and biddable, not at all like Mia.

Smiling at the comparison, Ayden scooped a measure of grain into the horse's feed trough, noted with some concern that the sleigh team were still absent from their stalls, and crossed the yard to the house. Light blazed through a window in the back door. He yanked it open and sighed with contentment at the heat and aromas of chicken soup, brewing coffee, and baking bread that surrounded him.

"You look frozen," his sister, Rosalie, greeted him from the stove. "Go change before you catch a chill."

"Thank you, Mom." He tugged one of Rosalie's dark curls tumbling down her back. "Where is Mom anyway?"

"Upstairs getting those poor children and their mother some dry clothes so we can feed them."

"So Pa has been home already? The team is gone."

"After he left the woman and the children here, he headed out again to see who else he could gather up." Rosalie set aside the spoon with which she stirred a pot of soup and faced him, her blue eyes dancing. "Where's Mia?"

Ayden suppressed a groan. "I should have known Pa would tell you all she's in town."

"He was bursting with the news."

"Such a vulgar expression. If you'd go to the college, you'd learn better—"

Rosalie whacked the back of his hand with her heavy wooden spoon. "Not tonight, Ayden." She tossed the spoon into the dry sink of dirty dishes and selected another one from a hook on the wall. "Go get yourself into dry clothes and come back for something hot to eat while you tell us all about Mia."

"Not tonight. Or any night. I'm too weary from pulling people out of railroad cars and need to get up to the church to see what else I can do to help."

"I'll go with you if Pa gets back. Fletcher has been at First Church since they started taking stranded passengers there." A smile played about her lips, and her eyes softened as she referred to the man who'd been courting her for nearly a year. "He asked me to come with him, but I didn't want to leave Mom home alone."

"Wise of you," Ayden said.

For once. He wouldn't say that aloud, even though the words spoke the truth.

Wisdom and common sense were not on the list of Rosalie's many good qualities. She was kind, intelligent, and beautiful. She also followed her heart more often than good judgment. Her adoration of Fletcher Lambert lay on the list of poor judgments.

But she was right. Tonight was not the time to poke at her about her future.

"I'm happy to hear Fletch is at the church," Ayden said. "It looked rather chaotic there."

"I expect it was worse at the wreck." Rosalie's eyes clouded. "Was it terrible?"

"It was unpleasant, but it could have been worse. I think we managed to save most everyone. If we didn't, they were beyond our help, I'm sad to say."

Rosalie gave him a sidelong glance, as she lifted a spoonful of soup to her lips. "Mia wasn't injured, was she?"

"Her wrist is hurting her."

Yet she had continued to seek that baby's people in spite of her pain. Mia would have sympathy for an abandoned child. She knew too much about abandonment.

Guilt pricked Ayden. He shook it off. She had left him, not the other way around.

Rosalie frowned at him. "If she's injured, you should have brought her here."

"She didn't want to come." Ayden turned away and started toward the inside kitchen door and paused there, his hand on the latch. "She wants no more to do with me than I want to do with her, so that's the end of it."

If only his heart would resume its normal operations instead of interfering with his breathing each time someone spoke Mia's name.

Chapter Three

*E*uphemia scowled at the bandage the doctor had wound around her left wrist, immobilizing it. "I'm not much use to anyone with only one free hand."

"You should be in a warm, dry bed with someone helping you, not the other way around," Dr. Clark told her. "If you don't get out of those wet clothes soon, a sprained wrist won't be your only trouble."

"Of course, Doctor. There's just one problem with that." Euphemia smiled sweetly. "I don't have any dry clothes."

"Then find a hot fire to stand in front of and steam yourself like a dumpling." He grinned despite the lines of fatigue etching his face, then he turned away to attend to a child with a woolen scarf wrapped around her foot instead of a shoe. "What happened here?"

"I loozed my shoe." The child's rosebud mouth quivered.

The sight reminded Euphemia of the toddler on the train, and she touched the doctor's shoulder. "I'm sorry to interrupt you, but have you tended a woman with a broken leg?"

He didn't look up as he began to unwind the scarf. "Nothing that serious yet. Looking for someone?"

"Yes, there was—"

Blood appeared on the pink yarn of the makeshift bandage, and the child started to wail, drowning Euphemia's words.

She glanced at the pale young woman with the child, guessing from the poor quality of her dress in comparison with the girl's thick wool and fur she was a nanny or governess rather than her mother. Mia decided not to ask her about the abandoned little boy. The young woman's pallor suggested she would be the doctor's next patient.

"Send a message to the boardinghouse if you encounter a woman with a broken leg," Euphemia said above the girl's cries of distress.

She turned and headed for the door of the church. Around her, passengers accepted blankets and dry clothes and cups of hot coffee and tea from townsfolk. The pastor of First Church offered the building for anyone who had no place to stay.

"Though we're getting crowded."

"So's the hotel," someone called. "Try the boardinghouse."

"I only have one room left, and it's reserved." Mrs. Greene, who had owned the boardinghouse practically from the founding of the town two decades earlier, stood in the doorway to the sanctuary. "If she don't show up in another ten minutes, I'm giving the room to someone else."

"I'm here." Euphemia wound her way around knots of people gathered in the entryway and reached out her right hand to the boardinghouse keeper. "I'm here, Mrs. Greene. Please don't give my room away."

"You can stay with us, Mia," Mr. Goswell said from behind her.

Euphemia smiled at him over her shoulder. "Thank you, but I'd rather you gave the space to people who truly need it."

"We already have," Mr. Goswell said. "That woman and her children will be staying in Frank's room."

He referred to their elder son, who now lived in Chicago.

"But we could put you up with Rosalie," he continued. "I wouldn't be able to put a stranger there."

"Of course you can't. But—" Euphemia cradled her injured wrist and writing case with her right arm. If Ayden weren't there, she would go in an instant. She always got along well with Rosalie. She adored Mrs. Goswell. Losing Ayden's family had been nearly as difficult as losing him—precisely why she could not stay in their house, accept their kindness and generosity of spirit. The hope she read in Mr. Goswell's face reminded her she must not give them the impression she would renew any sort of relationship with their son. She couldn't hurt them again any more than she wanted to be hurt again.

"I think we're all better off if I stay at the boardinghouse." She turned away and skirted a knot of people to reach the boardinghouse proprietress. "I'm here."

Mrs. Greene's eyes gleamed in her moon face. "I saw you. Gonna put you up in your old attic room. I know it's tiny, but I had to put families in the bigger rooms."

"That's quite all right." Euphemia tightened the corners of her mouth. "I'll pay the full rate." Before the woman could argue with her, Euphemia spun toward the door.

Mr. Goswell remained near the opening, and Ayden had joined him. So had a man and woman, each carrying a piece of luggage in one hand and holding the hand of a child with the other. The older Goswell male carried a piece of luggage. The younger one held a boy of perhaps five or six whose head lolled against Ayden's shoulder. His eyes met Euphemia's across the room, and at the sight of him holding a child so protectively in his arms, Euphemia felt as though the weight of one of those railroad cars were crushing her chest. If only things had gone differently, if only he had taken the teaching position in Boston instead of remaining in Hillsdale when the opportunity arose there, he could be holding their little boy like that in another few years. But he'd broken his promise and made a choice that took them in different directions, and her hope of having everything she wanted died in one spectacular razor-tongued dispute.

The scene blurred before Euphemia's eyes, and she turned away. She would exit the church through the back door.

She entered the sanctuary. People huddled together on the pews, many slumped or stretched out in repose, if not sleep. Volunteers from the town moved around, distributing blankets and cups of steaming liquids. Euphemia passed the little girl with the injured foot and the pallid governess. The former lay on the pew wrapped in a crocheted blanket, her bandaged toes sticking out. The latter sat beside her charge, her hands in darned black gloves and folded in her lap, her pale eyes fixed on the altar.

Euphemia nodded to the young woman and then slipped through the door beside the choir loft and away to the rear of the church. Little light save for the ambient reflection of snow shone through the window. The odor of burned candle wax and old songbooks stung her nostrils, scents as familiar to her as the college library but not as comforting. These aromas pricked her conscience.

She hadn't been to church in far too many weeks as she pursued and followed her dream—just like her father. Except she never made promises she didn't intend to keep. She would return to this church on Sunday and thank the Lord for preserving her life and that of so many others.

She opened the rear door to a blast of snow-thickened wind.

"Miss? Miss, a moment please?" The high, thin voice battled the whine of the wind around the corner of the building.

Euphemia slammed the door and turned back. "Yes?"

"May . . . may I speak with you a moment?" Light from the sanctuary shone on the pale hair and face of the governess.

Legs suddenly as stiff as a snow sculpture's, Euphemia retraced her steps down the passageway and joined the young woman just inside the church. "How may I help you?"

"I . . . well, I was wondering . . . I couldn't help but overhear . . ." The young woman twisted her hands together and gazed past Euphemia's left ear. "Some people offered you a place to stay, and I'm afraid my employers won't like me keeping their daughter amongst the hoi polloi.

That's what they'll call this." She swept one hand out to indicate the assembled persons sleeping on the pews. "But the hotel and boardinghouse are full. So I was wondering . . . we can compensate you, of course. My employers are generous when it comes to their daughter's needs."

"You'll compensate me for what?" Euphemia asked.

The young woman stared at Euphemia as though she were a rather dull-witted child. "Why, for you to give up your room in the boardinghouse and stay with your friends."

Euphemia's wrist throbbed. Her head ached. She could no longer feel her toes inside their sodden stockings and boots. She wanted nothing more than to steam herself dry beside a fire and then go to sleep in a real bed. But not a bed at the Goswell house. The strength to guard her heart against seeing Ayden, hearing Ayden, catching his scent of sandalwood and thyme and not suffering no longer ran through her veins.

She opened her mouth to say absolutely not, she needed that room to work, but the governess had begun twisting her hands together hard enough for her fingertip to protrude through one of the darns in her gloves. She must be poorly compensated or need her wages for other more important matters to wear such shabby gloves in the winter. The employers who were generous with their daughter's needs apparently didn't feel the same about her governess. Were they ungenerous enough to dismiss her for not taking good enough care of their daughter despite the circumstances?

The mere possibility kept Euphemia's mouth shut until she found the courage to answer. "All right. Tell Mrs. Greene you may have my room."

"Thank you." The young woman smiled, and her eyes glowed like sunlit silver. "I'll pray extra for you for this kindness." Back straight and steps light, she hastened to wake her young charge.

Euphemia retreated to the entryway. The Goswells had gone. She must, like a supplicant, arrive at their door in the middle of the night.

"How humiliating," she muttered.

The alternative, remaining at the church to sleep on a pew in her wet garments, was less acceptable. For warmth and food and a dry bed, she could swallow her pride just this once and risk encounters with Ayden—or perhaps not.

For several minutes, she stood in the doorway to the sanctuary, poised on her toes and uncertain whether to run up the aisle or out the front door. The sanctuary was warm enough. She would dry eventually beside the stove. Then again, Rosalie would lend her warm and comfortable garments in which to sleep. Ayden no longer assisted at the church and would be present at his home. On the other hand, the Goswell household seemed so crowded with stranded passengers that she should surely be able to avoid him.

The notion of comfort won in the end, and she headed down the street. Despite a new moon and the predawn hour, the lanterns hung outside houses and the glow of the snow lit her way along a route she knew well, a mere three blocks from the church.

In the night, the house looked the same—square and solid. Wood smoke scented the air around it, and a dog barked from beyond the front door.

Euphemia skirted the house to knock on the kitchen door. Ayden was less likely to be in the kitchen than the front parlor or study.

She was wrong. He opened the door.

"Mia." He jerked back a step. "I didn't think we'd see you again."

"I apologize. It wasn't my intention." She avoided looking at his deep-blue eyes, so warm in the cold night. "I gave up my place in the boardinghouse to a governess and her charge."

"You would." His voice held a tender note that brought tears to Euphemia's eyes.

She was tired was all, worn to a thread from the travel and the wreck and her aching wrist.

"You know you're welcome here." He waved to a brightly lit kitchen smelling of coffee and bread. "Come in."

Euphemia entered. Not until she pushed back her hood and shoved clumps of frozen hair out of her face did she notice the blonde seated at the table, peeling potatoes. She stood, revealing a trim figure in a merino dress over what had to be a crinoline to appear so crisp at that hour and a chignon without a hair out of place.

"This is Charmaine Finney," Ayden said. "A friend."

"You're a very good friend to be here helping in the middle of the night," Euphemia responded. "Pleased to meet you, Miss Finney." She pulled off her glove and held out her hand.

Miss Finney touched her fingertips. "When I heard how many people the Goswells had taken in, I just had to come and help. Father wouldn't have anyone in our house, I'm sad to say. He fears Mother's silver will disappear."

"Charmaine's father is now director of the Classics Department," Ayden said, as he closed the door.

What he didn't need to say was that the lovely lady's father was his director at the college.

"I remember Dr. Finney." Euphemia smiled at Ayden with the first genuine warmth she'd managed all night. She could afford to be friendly with him. "You should have told me you were taken. I wouldn't have worried about your parents trying to matchmake us."

"No, you shouldn't have to." His tone was brusque. "Let me find Momma and Rosalie. I think they're in the attic, digging up clothes for the children." He bolted from the kitchen like a schoolboy about to be caught in a naughty deed.

Euphemia raised her eyebrows. "I think I'll get myself some coffee and steam dry by the stove here, if you won't be inconvenienced by it." She removed her cloak and hung it on a hook by the door, beside several other wraps.

"Of course you will not inconvenience me. May I ladle you out some soup?"

"I think I am too weary to eat anything." Euphemia's head spun.

Miss Finney resumed peeling potatoes. "Do you know where to find cups, or should I help you?"

"I know where the cups are, if nothing's changed." Without releasing her left-armed hold on her writing case, Euphemia selected a thick mug from a cupboard and lifted the pot from the back of the stove.

The brew streamed into the cup, as thick and dark as oil. No doubt, the Goswells kept milk in the cellar this time of year, and she could fetch some to dilute the coffee, but she didn't bother. She needed the stimulating brew to keep her wits about her now that she stood in the Goswell home, now that she stood face-to-face with the new lady in Ayden's life.

Despite his vows of undying devotion to her, he had become involved with a new lady. Euphemia still woke aching with the loss of him, and he blithely courted another female.

You left him, she reminded herself.

But with good reason. His reasons for staying behind seemed moot now. Or were they? Gazing at Charmaine, Euphemia wondered if Ayden had found an easier road to his future than the one he had planned with her. What better way into the good graces of the director of a program in which Ayden wished to work than to court the head man's daughter?

Not that it must be a hardship. Charmaine was pretty. On second glance, she was beautiful, with her pale-blonde perfection, eyes the color of a summer lake, and skin as pure and smooth as that of a porcelain doll. Beside her looks, her attraction must also lie in her kindness. Not everyone would give up a night's sleep to help the Goswells prepare food for their household of unexpected guests.

The coffee turned to acid on Euphemia's lips and burned in her stomach, and she set the cup on the table, too weary to hold it any longer. She slumped in one of the kitchen chairs and held out her bandaged wrist. "I don't think I can help you peel potatoes, but maybe I can cut them."

"I think you should be in a bed, Miss Roper." Charmaine smiled. "Don't look so surprised. Of course I know who you are. My father talked about you when you were in his class as a freshman at Michigan Central College before it was Hillsdale College. He said you wrote the best papers of anyone, including Ayden."

"He was kind to me." Euphemia rested her head on her good hand. "But I don't remember you."

"I didn't go to the college. I attended a finishing school in Philadelphia." For a moment so brief Mia thought she must have imagined it, Charmaine's clear blue eyes clouded. Then she smiled, and the sun emerged again. "And now, I am Father's hostess and housekeeper and do some charity work for the church."

"And Ayden has made a good choice for his wife."

She wouldn't be running to a city to take on that unfeminine occupation—a career in journalism—or any other career beyond wife and mother, as Euphemia and a handful of other females did nowadays.

Charmaine laughed with a decided lack of humor. "Not quite that . . . yet."

The sound of voices outside the kitchen prevented Euphemia from saying more. She rose in time to meet Mrs. Goswell's voluminous, cinnamon-scented embrace.

"Mia. Oh, my, Mia Roper, you don't know how happy we are that you're here." The older woman drew back and wiped her eyes with the corner of her pristine apron. "We've prayed and prayed for you, and I knew I was right to know God promised you'd come back."

Euphemia refrained from saying God had nothing to do with her presence in their kitchen at four o'clock in the morning. At least she didn't think He did.

"I'm happy to see you, too, ma'am."

She was much happier now that Ayden's parents couldn't want her there for a reunion between her and Ayden, a painful prospect at best.

"You're drinking coffee to warm up?" Mrs. Goswell said. "I'll get you some soup and bread, too."

"She needs dry clothes first." Rosalie also embraced Euphemia. "Come up to my room, and I'll find you something. You're a little shorter and a little thinner than I am, but not by much." She slipped her arm through the crook of Euphemia's elbow and started for the door, then paused by Charmaine. "Thank you for doing all of those potatoes. Should Ayden walk you home?"

"I can stay if you need more help." Charmaine suppressed a yawn.

"You look tired after collecting all those blankets," Mrs. Goswell said. "But I'll have my husband take you in the sleigh. Not proper for you and Ayden to be out alone this time of the morning."

"And the snow looks deeper." Charmaine glanced to the doorway, where Ayden now stood.

The two shared a smile, and Euphemia closed her eyes.

Seeing the intimacy between Ayden and Charmaine should not hurt. She just wished "should not" and "did not" came out the same in the end. Unfortunately, her heart had wrapped itself around her windpipe, and each breath pained her.

Rosalie squeezed her arm. "Move out of the way, brother. This lady needs to change her dress."

"How's your wrist?" Ayden asked.

"Sprained and sore." Euphemia tried to smile and failed. "I'm managing."

"You always did." He moved away from the door and strode to stand behind Charmaine's chair. "If there aren't any classes tomorrow, which I doubt there will be . . ."

Rosalie nearly dragged Euphemia from the kitchen, allowing the door to bang shut behind her. "If there aren't classes tomorrow, he'll bring her back here to help Momma cook, and we'll all be miserable."

Euphemia blinked. "You don't like her? She seems like a nice lady." "She is." Rosalie paused with one foot on the bottom step. "She is sweet and pretty and giving and kind and just so good at everything she makes the rest of us feel like a herd of elephants in a crystal room." "Ah, no wonder Ayden is taken with her." Euphemia managed the words in a neutral voice.

Rosalie snorted. "He is taken with the notion of being married to the daughter of someone who can get him the position he wants at the college."

"Ayden would never be that mercenary." Euphemia's defense of Ayden emerged in a flash. At once, she called herself a hypocrite since she had thought much the same thing mere moments earlier.

"I would like to think that about my brother, but I'm not entirely sure sometimes." Rosalie started up the steps. "You'll share my room. I have a blazing fire and warm things for you, and I'll bring you up a tray so you don't have to see my brother until you feel more yourself."

"Do I have to see your brother at all?"

"Oh, I do hope so." Rosalie turned right at the top of the polished wood steps and headed along a strip of red Turkish carpet to the end of the hallway. At the last room on the left, she pushed open the door to a room with a fire crackling in the small hearth and a dressing gown and slippers toasting over a chair before the blaze. "Now that you're here, Mom and Pa and I all hope he will change his mind about making an offer for Miss Charmaine Finney's hand in marriage and come to his senses about you."

"Um, no, Rosalie." Euphemia stumbled into the pink-and-white bedroom and held her free hand out to the flames. "I didn't come back here to renew anything with Ayden. I'm strictly here for work. If not for the wreck, I would have avoided seeing any of you at all." She ducked her head. "I am sorry to say that after you all were such a family to me, but what was between Ayden and me is obviously over."

"Ha. You went all stiff down there when Ayden looked at her." Rosalie adjusted a carved wooden screen across one corner. "Go in there and change into this nightgown and robe. Then I can tell you why your arrival is such an answer to prayer."

Euphemia didn't move. "I don't want to hear any such thing. I wouldn't interfere with Ayden and his fiancée, even if I still wanted him to court me, which I do not. He hurt me too much."

"I know he did. But, Mia"—Rosalie grasped Euphemia's hand between both of hers and gazed at her with the Goswell blue eyes, rich in color, intense with emotion—"if I thought Ayden loved Charmaine, I would make sure you didn't interfere with their courtship. But he doesn't."

"He didn't love me either, obviously." Euphemia blinked back moisture in her eyes. "You know that."

Despite the seven years' difference in their ages, Euphemia had wept on Rosalie's shoulder a year and a half ago.

Rosalie sighed. "I know he was beastly to you. I didn't speak to him for weeks after you left and he didn't. But, Mia, him marrying Charmaine would be worse. She is a nice person, but he's courting her for all the wrong reasons, even if he won't admit it."

Chapter Four

Ayden rested his elbows on the kitchen table, too weary to move, too awake to go to bed. At five o'clock in the morning, he may as well stay awake. He needed to shovel snow. The horses also needed to be fed and their stalls mucked out. With all the soup she'd heated and coffee she'd brewed during the night, Ma would need more wood chopped for the stove.

Most of Hillsdale might call him Professor Goswell, but he was still Wilson and Rebecca Goswell's younger son, who was living at home, and as such, he was expected to help with the chores. He tried to execute those chores before he headed for campus at seven thirty in the morning. Otherwise, he found himself wielding an ax and splitter between preparing lectures and grading tests. That didn't work so well when he arrived at class with wood shavings clinging to his coat and hair. Students, especially the female ones, concentrated more on his disheveled appearance than his history lectures. The young women vied for custody of his overcoat to brush it clean. More than one young lady had tried to brush his hair for him. Being no more than ten years older than the students, he needed to watch his step with the women, gently reminding them they had come to get an equal education with the male students, an opportunity less than half a dozen colleges in the country offered.

Too often, his subtle reminders of the young ladies' purpose in attending Hillsdale College failed him. No matter how often he made it clear he was the professor, not a potential husband, numerous women students persisted in leaving cookies, pies, and even a layer cake in his office. They weren't trying to bribe him to give them better grades. Most were perfectly capable of earning those grades all on their own. They did not, however, hesitate in their attempts to earn his attention outside the classroom.

God bless Charmaine for coming along with her sweet nature and blonde beauty. During the past few months of their courtship, the gifts of baked goods had dwindled, though a few trickled in from time to time.

Of course, discouraging the female student population from flirting with him was not the only reason he'd begun to court Charmaine. He enjoyed her company, her serenity, her kindness. Never in his life had he been so comfortable in the presence of a female, including Mia.

Mia was anything but a comfortable female to be around. She voiced opinions. She argued. She set out to accomplish a task and wasn't always careful about how she got there.

But he had loved her to distraction. He had wept when she left Hillsdale with a vow never to return. So now, when he was all but engaged to Charmaine, Mia reneged on her promise to never see him again and leaped off that wrecked train.

"Now what do I do?" He didn't realize he had cried out in a moment of desperation until a hand dropped onto his shoulder.

"You might want to try a few hours of sleep," Ma suggested.

Ayden smiled up at her. "Too much to do. The horses, the shoveling, avoiding Mia."

"That's going to be rather difficult." Ma went to the stove and began to make coffee. "This is a fine, big house, but it's not that big. Unless you stay away from dawn to bedtime, you're bound to see her."

"I've got plenty of work to keep me away." He rose. "I'll see to the horses and the shoveling."

"You don't want some coffee and breakfast first?"

"It'll taste even better after hard work in the cold."

Maybe the physical labor would clear his head of the image of Mia's arresting face surrounded by the snow-crusted fur trimming her hood. It was surely the same hood that had surrounded her face on many a ride in the sleigh or on a sledding expedition like the one when he first kissed her until her lips were no longer stiff from cold, until they glowed as rosy as her cheeks and were warm enough to melt falling snowflakes.

His own cheeks suddenly far too warm, he stamped his feet into his boots and stalked from the house, away from the heat and into the cold. He closed the door behind him, wishing he could so easily close the door on memories of how happy Euphemia Roper had made him before that first kiss, during those glorious moments, and long afterward.

"Think about Charmaine." He spoke the words aloud, then repeated them.

While raking soiled straw from the horses' stalls, he focused on Charmaine's face, her curls the color of ripe wheat, her eyes the color of the sky on a clear day in August, the luscious strawberry hue of her lips—lips he hadn't yet kissed. Maybe he should. Maybe that would once and for all drive memories of Mia from his head.

But he couldn't get Mia out of his head while she slept under his parents' roof.

He forked fresh straw into stalls and hay into mangers with so much vigor the carriage team backed against the walls of their stalls as if they expected him to grab their manes with the tines and haul them behind the stable. His own mount snorted and stamped, as though more than a little sympathetic.

"Charmaine is restful." Ayden grabbed the shovel and attacked the snow drifting across the walkways. "She will make a perfect hostess."

He flung snow into piles Rosalie would no doubt diminish to produce one of her snowmen. "She's had a great deal of practice."

She had played hostess for her father since her mother's death a year earlier. And Dr. Finney entertained a great deal, as the director of the Classics Department at the college was expected to do. Ayden should attend because he was the newest lecturer awaiting Finney's approval for the position to become permanent.

A shovelful of snow sailed off the walk and struck the kitchen window, then tumbled atop one of Ma's lilac bushes. Two branches snapped beneath the onslaught.

Ma yanked open the back door. "I think you've done enough shoveling, Ayden. You should get yourself in here and warm up before you do any more damage."

"Yes, ma'am." He set the shovel beside the back door, then gathered an armload of firewood before shouldering his way into the kitchen.

The aromas of fresh-brewed coffee, fried ham and potatoes, and baked apples and cinnamon caused his mouth to water and his stomach to growl. After dumping the firewood into the box, he removed his boots and coat and crossed the room to slide a stack of plates from the cupboard. "Should I set these in the dining room for you?"

"Thank you, and get a fire going." Ma didn't look up while flipping sliced potatoes in a skillet. "Then maybe you could go wake up that sleepyhead sister of yours."

Ayden paused in the doorway and faced his mother with a shake of his head. "I don't think that's a good idea."

"Why not?" Ma drew her silver-flecked eyebrows together.

Ayden let the kitchen door swing shut behind him. She would work it out. If the creak of floorboards overhead was any indication, Rosalie was already awake. She must be trying to let Mia sleep, since no voices drifted through the ceiling plaster. Kind of her, but then Rosalie was nothing if not kind. If only she'd go to the college or find a beau more worthy of her lively goodness.

He set the plates on the table with a clatter of crockery, then stooped before the hearth. A fire had been laid. All he needed to do was crumple newspaper and wood shavings atop the logs and set a match to the kindling. They ignited with a whoosh and blaze of heat. He held his hands to the warmth while cold cloaked his back. The kitchen was far warmer, yet Rosalie's voice, sparkling like sun-dappled water, told him she spoke of Mia.

"I think her wrist is paining her, and we should make her stay in bed. She looks so tired and sad. I don't think the city agrees with her."

"It's a long journey," Ma pointed out. "And with the wreck, she's probably a bit overwrought."

Not to mention seeing him again. Or maybe it was arrogant of him to think encountering him had any effect on her at all.

He rose and returned to the kitchen. In the event Mia did rise for breakfast, he should make matters easier for her and vacate the house.

He pushed open the door in time to see Rosalie tipping a few drops of laudanum into a cup of tea. She startled at his entrance, and a few more drops splashed into the cup.

"What are you doing?" His tone was mild, his look sharp.

Rosalie shrugged. "You know Mia. Unless she's changed a great deal, she'll be insisting she get up unless we make her sleep."

"Shouldn't you let her choose whether or not she wishes to be drugged?" Ayden reached for the cup.

Rosalie snatched it out of his reach. "She's in pain from her wrist. The doctor recommended a few drops, but she wouldn't let me get up for it last night."

"Ayden is right." Ma reached for a clean cup. "You shouldn't give her medicine without her knowing."

"All right. I'll ask her." Rosalie's lips turned down. "But if she says no and then ends up dashing around town and hurting herself worse, it'll be on your head, brother."

"If she says yes," Ayden countered, "we'll know she's seriously hurt and maybe needs to see the doctor again."

And if she said no, he needed to make himself scarce.

He strode to the back door and got his boots and coat. "I'm off to see if I can look for clues about that child's people at the wreck, and then I'll be on the campus."

"There aren't any classes today." Ma cast him a narrow-eyed glance. "Do you plan to move into the museum while she's here?"

"That sounds wise."

Or make Miss Finney an offer of marriage sooner than he had planned.

He stamped his feet into his boots. "I have some weapons to examine and oil and two students to tutor."

"You and your tutoring." Rosalie balanced a tray of tea and toast on her hip. "I'm surprised Charmaine endures it with such grace."

"Miss Finney," Ayden said, "endures everything with grace." He yanked on his coat and left the house.

He couldn't go out to the wreck this early. The sun had not yet risen, and he couldn't take the horses into the cold so soon after they had eaten. He would head up to the campus. The museum, where he kept his collection of ancient weapons, always gave him shelter. He could lose himself in the work there for hours.

Which he did. Between oiling each blade with loving care and making a few notes on blade details to ensure no erosion of the metal was taking place, and three interruptions by students anxious about their assignments, most of the day sped by him. One of his tutees was doing so well she was unlikely to need his help much longer. The other one, a male student, needed to play less baseball and read more history.

When Ayden was about to close the museum and head out to the wreck, his third tutee appeared in the museum doorway.

"This is Gerrett Divine." Blushing, the student, Liberty Judd, indicated her companion. "He needs some vellum to recopy some plans that were lost in the wreck." She flashed a glance at Divine, then back to Ayden. "He is an architect, a family friend I have known all my life."

From her blush and glance, Ayden suspected Gerrett Divine was more than a friend to Miss Judd. She did not need a distraction from her schoolwork at that point in the semester. She had little enough aptitude for formal education, though she was bright and lively and pretty enough to charm anyone. Perhaps Divine would help her decide whether she should buckle down to her studies or return to her family in the city.

Ayden turned his attention to Divine. "I probably have some vellum you can have, though you may need to scrape it clean of ink." He glanced at Miss Judd. "Where is he staying?"

"The boardinghouse." She sounded a little breathless.

All she needed were more distractions like Divine staying under the same roof as she did.

"Why don't you come stay with us, Mr. Divine," Ayden suggested. "We already have five guests, but we can make more room."

He could vacate his chamber and bunk down in the attic schoolroom. It wouldn't be all that comfortable, but its location and another guest in the house would make evading Mia that much easier.

"Thank you." Divine inclined his head. "I know Mrs. Greene would like to give my room to a family, and it does seem like a waste for me to have all that space to myself under the circumstances."

"Very good, then."

Ayden dug up some vellum left over from invitations to the Valentine's festivities to be held in another few days, then he headed down the hill and into town. On his way along Broad Street, he came abreast a wagon laden with luggage, some of which appeared somewhat singed, all of which appeared battered. Most had obviously been exposed to moisture.

"They managed to salvage some luggage," he called up to the driver.

The driver nodded. "A bit. Taking it to the church for people to claim what's theirs."

"I'll come along then and see if any belongs to those people staying with us."

"Climb aboard." The driver patted the seat beside him.

Ayden swung onto the board. "You haven't heard of anyone who's lost a child, have you?"

"No, sir. Seems like an important bit of luggage to lose." The driver guided the draft horses around the point onto Howell. "Why'd you ask?"

Ayden explained.

The man's pale-brown eyes creased at the corners, while a scarf hid most of the bottom half of his wind-burned face. "Never heard the like. But I'll be asking around."

"Please do. Report anything you learn to me. I'm Ayden Goswell."

They reached First Church, and Ayden spent the next hour helping to distribute luggage while inquiring after the lost child's people. Too little baggage had survived the wreck and fire, and many people turned away from the piles of bags with stricken faces.

Ayden departed with his own disappointment to have learned nothing about the little boy. He trudged home carrying Mia's rather battered portmanteau and entered the house to find nearly everyone assembled in the parlor reading, playing a board game, or dozing by the fire.

"You are late," Mom said.

"Whose luggage is that?" Rosalie leaped to her feet. "Did you go out to the wreck?"

"No, I got this at First Church." Ayden set the case in the front hall. "It's Mi—Euphemia's."

The woman from the train, whose name Ayden still did not know, glanced his way, then toward the toddler, who was squeezing a lumpy stuffed dog on the carpet. "Did you learn anything about him?" Her voice was whispery, and she did not meet his eyes.

He shook his head. "It's like someone simply dropped the child onto the train and forgot about him. No one noticed him or anyone with him."

"Did you ask about the woman with the injured leg?" Mia spoke from behind him, her voice low, like cool, soothing fingers on a fevered brow.

A thrill ran up his spine. His shoulders stiffened. He must not respond to her this way. She had betrayed him before. She was perfectly clear now that she was only in Hillsdale on a temporary assignment. If he didn't look at her, he wouldn't care that she stood in his home.

But everyone was looking at him, including the children in the middle of the floor.

He turned and took in her appearance in a glance. She had always looked delicate. Now she looked fragile, as though a medium breeze would knock her over. The multitude of petticoats belling out her soft wool skirt emphasized how thin she was, far thinner than she had been when Ma had been feeding her five out of seven nights a week.

"Don't they feed you in Boston?" he asked.

Pa chuckled. Ma and Rosalie gasped.

"You're so rude," Rosalie scolded. "She's as beautiful as ever."

Mia smiled and cradled her left wrist with her other hand. "I work hard and don't have cooking as fine as Mrs. Goswell's to sustain me." She glanced at Rosalie. "And I'll be wary of younger sisters bearing gifts of food and tea in the future."

Ayden glared at his sister. "You didn't ask her about the laudanum?"

"I, um,"—Rosalie bit her lip—"well, I said it was just a drop or two."

"Rosalie, that's—"

"She meant well." Mia glided forward, her skirts rustling, her head high, though her neck seemed too thin to support so much hair. "I'm sure I needed the rest, but I would have liked to have gone looking for the boy's mother."

"He doesn't even have a name," the little girl said. "We just call him Boy."

"The quality of his clothes is fine," Ma said. "I sent them out with the laundry. They were filthy."

"Did they have any initials in them?" Ayden asked.

At the same time, Mia asked, "Were they monogrammed?"

They looked at one another. Their eyes met in a flash of remembered camaraderie, for they had often spoken the same thoughts.

Ayden jerked back a step. "I'm going to Charmaine's. They're expecting me for dinner."

"You should stay home." Pa levered himself from his chair with the stiffness he had shown since his accident two years earlier. "We have that young man you invited to stay here coming." He started to stoop to add more logs to the fire.

Ayden strode over and crouched before the blaze to do the task instead. "I'll chop some more wood before I go."

He needed the exercise and the immediate escape from the faint whiff of lemon verbena—Mia's scent.

"The Taggart boy chopped plenty today." Pa returned to his chair and lowered himself into it with a slowness that made Ayden's back hurt to watch. "You run off if you must tonight, but tomorrow, I think you should help Mia hunt for that boy's people."

"He need not," Mia protested.

"I really should be making lesson plans up on the hill." Ayden referred to the college, his retreat, his escape, his lame excuse for not helping Mia. With his family giving him accusing glares, he turned away. "I should be going."

"Running off." Rosalie's taunting voice rang after Ayden all the way down the street to the Finney house.

So what if he was. A prudent man ran away from trouble. And being near Mia was trouble.

With her staying in his parents' house, he couldn't run away from trouble in the form of coming face-to-face with Euphemia Roper. What had he been thinking to invite her to stay there? He should have known his heart would suffer. Yet he thought he had been healed of that pain, believed offering her accommodations far more comfortable than the boardinghouse was the right thing to do. And Pa had insisted. He was courting Charmaine Finney, and if he didn't love her with the same devotion he had given Mia, that was the safer course for his future. Charmaine did not possess the power to wound his heart as Mia had.

Though he thought he could escape the house early to avoid taking Mia to hunt for the lost child's people, she was up early with Ma. He rose from building up the dining room fire, turned toward the doorway, and Mia stood there before him, one arm balancing a tray laden with silverware and cups.

The sun hadn't yet risen, but firelight limned her face, making her skin glow and drawing red highlights from her chestnut hair. She wore that hair braided and wound around her head, a severe style that emphasized her delicate bones and the dark shadows beneath her green eyes.

"You should be resting." He removed the tray from her hand, his glance dropping to her bandaged wrist. "No portfolio this morning?"

She looked past his shoulder. "I don't usually eat with it."

"That's not what I recall."

A stab of pain struck him the instant he read hurt on her face.

They'd fought about that once. He wanted her full attention during a picnic, and she wanted to write down her impressions of some incident she had witnessed in town before she forgot them. He could not understand how the sight of a policeman and a shopkeeper chasing a ragged boy with a basket of strawberries was more important than paying attention to him. Mia had given him a scathing glance, murmured something about how he had never wanted for anything, and continued to write, much as he had found her the night of the train wreck.

He should have known during that picnic that their future together was doomed.

He should have known better now than to bring up the subject. He should apologize. Instead, he turned toward the table. "Has all that writing not paid off well enough for you to now be famous?"

She did not respond, for which he did not blame her. The query did not deserve an answer. It was mean, born of a hurt he thought he no longer felt.

"I am sorry," he said.

When he still received no response, Ayden turned to see Mia had left the dining room. He sighed. He deserved her silent abandonment. Without her presence, the room felt colder.

Seeking nothing more than warmth and food, he followed Mia into the kitchen. Heat, the scent of fresh ground pepper on the potatoes, and female voices swirled around him. "So what do you plan to do today?" Ma was asking.

"Work." Mia lifted slices of fried ham from the skillet and slid them onto a platter. "Rosalie should be down any minute. I'm not sure about the lady with the children and that little boy I took off the train. Should I go up and wake them?"

"Let them sleep," Ayden said at the same time as his mother.

"I can keep food warm for them in the oven," Ma added. She pulled open the oven door and lifted out a sheet of biscuits. "Once we're done cooking here. Ayden, take this platter into the dining room."

Ayden took the platter of fried potatoes from Ma. "I'd rather fix a plate for myself and eat in here. It's warmer."

"The dining room will be warm soon enough, and there's not enough room in here." Ma pointed her spatula at the table only large enough for two. "Now take that platter in and come back for Mia's plate."

"I can manage." Mia lifted the platter with one hand, but it tilted far enough for a slice of meat to slide onto the worktable. She set the platter down again as her face flooded with hot color. "I'm sorry. My wrist should be better in a day or two, the doctor told me."

"I'll get it." Ayden took her platter in his other hand. "With the way you hang on to that portfolio of yours, you would think you would have hurt your other wrist."

"Ayden." Ma rapped his knuckles with her spatula as though he were a small boy stealing sweets. "That was unkind."

Mia fingered her wrist but looked Ayden in the eye. "I probably wouldn't have hurt my wrist if I'd been holding on to my portfolio."

"Likely you'd have bumped your head instead, which might have—" He stopped.

The days of gentle teasing were over. After his rather unkind remark about her holding on to her portfolio, a remark about a blow on her head knocking sense into her, a remark too easily taken wrong, was not the right conversational gambit.

"I'm glad nothing's broken." He swung around and marched into the dining room in time to hear a giggle and a whisper and the patter of small feet on the steps.

"Come on in here," he called to the children.

A boy and girl peeked around the edge of the dining room door. He hadn't paid much attention to them before. They looked near three years apart in age, but their relationship to one another was apparent in their big brown eyes and wild black curls.

"Hungry?" Ayden asked.

They nodded.

"Is your mother coming?" he pressed.

They nodded again, then the girl whispered, "She's bringing that boy without a momma."

"How did he lose his momma?" the boy asked.

"I don't know, but I'm going to keep looking for his momma today." Ayden pulled out a chair and bowed to the little girl. "We all need breakfast first. Will you sit here, Miss—?" He raised an eyebrow.

"Herring," the girl said. "Ellie Herring, and this is my brother, Roy."

"Well, then, Miss and Mr. Herring, come join us." Ayden pulled out another chair. "Do you like milk?"

Ma bustled into the room, carrying a tray filled with a milk jug, glasses, and a coffeepot. "Did you children wash your hands?"

They nodded and held up tiny hands.

"Good. We'll get you some help until your momma gets down." Ma cast Ayden a questioning glance.

"They tell me she's helping that lost child get ready."

Chattering away like a squirrel protecting his walnut tree, Rosalie entered the dining room, towing Mrs. Herring behind her. She carried the child Mia had rescued after the wreck, the one without a mother. Either without or, worse, abandoned by his mother. The child was too young to say one way or another. But he did not seem distraught to be surrounded by strangers. When Mrs. Herring took the chair between her own children, the little boy sat on her lap, his head resting against her shoulder, his thumb poked between puckered lips.

Mia entered with a basket of biscuits, and Ma motioned for Ayden to help her bring in the rest of the food. Pa and Gerrett Divine arrived in the middle of the serving, and for several minutes, organized chaos reigned. Once all the food rested on the table, everyone was seated, and the blessing was spoken, Ayden found Mia across the breakfast table from him.

For months before their engagement crashed to a conclusion, he had imagined this moment of having Mia across from him in the morning. The two of them would share a pot of coffee, deliberately brush fingers as they handed one another butter or jelly. They would talk about what the newspapers had printed and what they needed to read, study, or otherwise accomplish that day . . . In his dream, they would be alone, however, and her hair would be loose on her shoulders. She would smile at him with sleepy joy.

Seeing her with her hair wound tight, her face drawn, not joyful, and the crowd of strangers around them, his heart felt bruised all over again. She hadn't even spoken to him since their last exchange in the kitchen.

No, not exchange. His last comment to her.

No longer hungry, he drained his coffee and pushed back his chair. "If I may please be excused, I'd like to get going on looking for that baby's mother."

"I need to be doing the same." Mia looked at him then and pushed back her own chair. She set her napkin beside a plate with little food spooned onto it and barely any of it touched.

Ma frowned, looking from one to the other. "Neither of you has eaten enough for going into the cold."

"I don't need much breakfast." Mia flashed her quick, warm smile at Ma.

Pa chuckled. "Or lunch or dinner, by the look of you, young lady."

Her smile flashed for Pa this time. "I can't take the time to eat. I have already lost a day. Right now, I need to work."

"When don't you need to work?" The words slipped out from Ayden's lips before he could stop himself. Against the background of the children's chatter and the smell of rich food and wood smoke, that remark sounded bitter.

Mia met his gaze straight on and smiled at him, this time without the warmth. "I need to work as often as you do, Professor Goswell."

Which was why their dreams of marital bliss had been doomed from the start.

He took a deep breath to ease the tightness in his chest. "Then go get yourself some warm clothes, and we'll be off."

"You don't need to escort me," Mia insisted. "I travel all over the East Coast without an escort."

"But you shouldn't." Ma's chin took on its stubborn set. "I'd say you'd be all right here, but with all these extra people in town, I'll feel more comfortable having you in Ayden's company."

"Yes, ma'am." A flash in Mia's eyes belied the humility of her response. Head bowed, she slipped from the room and vanished up the steps.

Ayden sighed. "Ma, please don't try to matchmake us. I am all but engaged to Miss Finney."

"Or to that position at the college," Rosalie murmured.

"Rosalie, mind your tongue." Pa gave Ayden one of his gentle but stern looks. "The least you can do for that young lady is help her today."

"The least I can do for her—" Mindful of curious glances from Divine and Mrs. Herring, Ayden turned toward the kitchen door.

"Brother?" Rosalie called after him.

He glanced back. "Yes, sister?"

She scowled at him. "If you don't make hay when the sun shines this time, I'll never forgive you."

Ayden stalked into the kitchen. By the time he donned boots and coat, hat and gloves, Mia had arrived in the kitchen with her face surrounded by white fur and that portfolio tucked beneath her arm.

He sighed. "Of course it's coming along."

Rather like a third person on an outing for a courting couple. At least it had been that way before. If they were still courting, or even married, apparently it would be that way again.

"Let's go." He offered her his arm.

She didn't take it until they reached the street. Wearing boots looking far more fashionable than useful, she slipped in snow packed by prior feet and sleigh runners. She clung to his forearm, her hand small and strong. Though her wide skirt swirled around his legs with each step, she said nothing to him. A glance down told him she didn't even look at him. She kept her head bowed as though she was praying. Or perhaps she merely watched her feet, and clutched that portfolio to her front like a shield.

"It always was, wasn't it?" he mused aloud.

She glanced up, her cheeks pink in the cold. "What?"

"That notebook of yours always was a shield between us. You cover your heart with it like you expect me to stab it."

"Or twist the knife you stuck in it eighteen months ago."

"Ouch."

She turned her head away, then stopped, a gasp forming vapor from her breath.

He followed her gaze to where the rising sun shimmered on pristine snow and icicles dripping from trees and eaves like diamond crystals. It was a sight Ayden saw so often he didn't think about its beauty. In truth, by February, he'd had enough of winter for the year. Tramping up the hill to the college grew tiresome. Now, however, seeing it from Mia's perspective, the glory of a sunrise over snow and ice became a fresh vision, a reminder that he had once viewed the display as a promise.

He spun away. "We need to get going." He started walking without warning.

She stumbled after him, clinging harder to his arm. "And where are you dragging me?"

"You wanted to come."

"I have an editor expecting articles from me. Of course I wanted to come."

She didn't want to come because of him. Good. That was the way it needed to be. This reappearance of hers should be one last reminder to him that her desire to be a journalist was more important to her than anything they had shared.

"So you are working with a periodical?" He made himself ask the question as any former classmate might.

"I'm writing individual pieces, but if I do well with this assignment, I'll be hired as a regular reporter." Her voice sparkled like the icicles in the sunrise.

"It's what you always wanted."

They reached Howell Street, and he turned toward the church. "We can begin here. No one knew anything yesterday, but things might have changed this morning."

Suddenly, Mia jerked her hand from his arm and strode away from him. A score of feet away, she swung to face him so quickly her wide skirt lifted in the wind and her hood slipped onto her shoulders. "I can go into the church and ask. Unless you plan to go out to the wreck itself, there's no need for us to stay together."

She headed up the steps. Still watching her abrupt departure, Ayden did not notice Charmaine and her father until they halted on the pavement in front of him.

"Ayden." Charmaine's smile was bright, but strain tightened the porcelain skin around her eyes. "You look so tired still. Did you get enough sleep last night?"

"Too little, I'm afraid." He took her gloved hand in his and bowed over it.

It was leather as soft as butter. Everything about Charmaine was soft and sweet, from her hands to her voice to her big blue eyes. Yes, and her heart as well. He adored her.

He just wished he loved her.

He wished he liked her father. Dr. Finney, in contrast to his daughter, was anything but soft. His face was etched in hard lines. His blue eyes resembled something about as yielding as sapphires. Even his physique appeared hard, although he was in his fifties. Students said Finney was carved of stone, not human flesh.

Except where it came to his daughter. He smiled down at her now and patted her hand. "Would you like to invite Professor Goswell to our house for coffee and some of that cake you made? It is sure to make him feel better, just from the smell."

Charmaine laughed and blushed. "Papa, you are so droll." She turned back to Ayden. "It would be lovely of you to come by. Some of the other professors are coming over for refreshment and maybe a look at that Egyptian paper someone has acquired."

"Papyrus, child." Finney sighed as he corrected his daughter.

Ayden would love to get a look at the scroll, even though medieval weaponry was his favorite type of history. And Charmaine's cakes tasted better than anyone else's in town, including the baker's.

He shook his head with regret. "I'm afraid I'll have to indulge myself with one of your cakes at another time. I have work to do to help the wreck victims."

"What sort of work?" Finney's voice rang like an ax on stone. "It's bad enough your parents saw fit to take half a dozen of those people into your house, but for you to be expected to help is not acceptable."

Ayden ground his teeth behind a plastered on smile. "I am not expected to help. I've chosen to help."

"Is that Miss Roper I see going into the church?" Charmaine broke in a little too quickly. "I can't believe I didn't recognize the name last night. But I picked up one of my ladies' magazines after you left last night, and there was an article by her about women going into nursing."

"Vulgar." Finney wrinkled his nose as though the idea were also noisome.

"She's proud of women who find careers of their own," Charmaine persisted.

"Hardly sounds like fit company for you, Charmaine."

An odd remark from a man who worked at a college dedicated to giving women the same educational opportunities as men.

Ayden thought perhaps he should defend his female students, if he would not defend Mia. But with the decision about the full-time professorship imminent, now was not the time to raise the ire of the Classics Department director.

Finney stomped his feet. "Standing here in the cold is not acceptable either. Let's deliver those pastries and be on our way home." Another indulgent smile for his daughter. "She insisted on bringing some pastries to the church."

"That's kind of you." Ayden kept his gaze on Charmaine. "And I do apologize for turning down your kind invitation, but I have to find the mother of that little boy we took in."

"That." Finney made a chopping gesture with his right fist. "You should bring him here to the church and let the town council find a home for him. Then you can come to our house and accomplish something more useful than associating with the train riffraff—like securing your future at the college."

Chapter Five

꧁ᴥ꧂

*I*ce spotted the church steps, and Mia took her time ascending. The last thing she wanted to do was fall on her face in front of Ayden and the Finneys. On the other hand, not overhearing the dialogue on the pavement might have been worth the risk of humiliating herself, especially the last bit. As she turned to close the church door, Mia caught the words of Dr. Finney regarding train riffraff and noticed his eyes fixed upon her. She pursed her lips to avoid the childish impulse to stick her tongue out at him.

"I graduated from your precious college, Dr. Finney," she muttered through her clenched teeth. "You thought I was an excellent student."

She had never liked Tobias Finney. She liked him even less when he took over the Classics Department, as he was the reason why Ayden had stayed behind instead of coming to Boston with her. He had invited the brilliant young scholar to join the faculty at the college, when it reformed as Hillsdale College, until they could fill the position with someone more qualified to make the position permanent.

Now the time had come to fill the position with a full-time professor, and Ayden was the front-runner for the permanent position. Marriage to the director's daughter, according to Rosalie, would ensure

Ayden acquired his lifelong dream of becoming a history professor with little fear of not having work the next year.

And if Mia didn't get her articles written, she wouldn't achieve her dream of becoming a journalist earning a salary instead of one paid whenever the editor chose to buy one of her articles. She would be forced to continue with her if not Spartan, far from secure existence, making enough money to live on however she could in a respectable manner.

The train wreck was not, of course, her assignment. It would, however, make a fine addition to the story about how Hillsdale College allowed female students to study right alongside male students. Most institutions of higher education considered women incapable of learning the same subjects at the same time in the same classroom with men.

"We proved them wrong." With a smug little smile curving her lips, Mia strode into the church. Her right hand gripped a pencil. Her left balanced her open portfolio, ready for receiving notes on what she saw.

Chaos. Not as much as the night of the wreck, but there were still far too many people crowding the entryway and sanctuary, children crying, women looking like they wanted to weep, and men with faces a little too stony to be their natural expressions. They were stranded hours from any city of note, without proper shelter, food, or clothing. The room stank of wet wool, babies needing to be changed, and hot soup. She wondered when these people would be able to continue along their journeys. The railroad men would have to answer that.

Visit depot, she added to her list of impressions.

She began to move around, jotting down snippets of dialogue. "Momma, is my doll burned up?"

"What do you expect me to do, build you a house right here and now?"

"I just want to sleep."

A hand caught at her skirt, halting Mia in her tracks. "Help me."

She looked down at an older woman perched on a low chair. "What do you need?"

"Something to eat." Rheumy eyes moved behind rimless spectacles. "I couldn't get to the line when they served the food."

"And no one's with you?" Mia's gaze strayed around the room in search of someone from the town aiding those stranded in the church.

She saw no one she recognized except for Ayden coming through the front door with Miss Finney. The latter's smile appeared a bit stiff, and she pressed her back against the wall beside the door while Ayden carried a basket toward a table that still bore the decimated remains of toast and porridge.

Mia raised her right hand, still clutching the pencil, and waved to him, then dropped her gaze back to the diminutive old lady. "I'll get someone to help you. Were you traveling alone?"

"On my way to see my daughter in Chicago." The lady smiled, showing a fine set of porcelain teeth. "She's having her eleventh child."

"How . . . prodigious of her." Mia shuddered at the notion of so many children breaking into her thoughts and work.

"I wondered what happened to you." Ayden appeared beside her, his nearness reminding her that she hadn't always felt that way about children. Once upon a time, the mere echo of that deep, resonant voice sent shivers of anticipation down her spine.

But "once upon a time" belonged in fairy tales, which weren't real—just like their love.

She swallowed against a suddenly dry throat. "This lady hasn't eaten. Apparently getting to the food line is too difficult for her. I thought that basket might have some food in it."

"Quite a lot." Ayden crouched to be at eye level with the lady. "I have some apple fritters and some muffins. Would one apiece be enough, or would you like two?"

"Just one or the other." Tension around the lady's eyes vanished as though she were a drawing and the artist had taken an eraser to the tightness.

"Two apiece—to tide you over." Ayden wrapped the pastries in a sheet of newsprint and handed them over. "And there's the reverend bringing out more coffee. Would you like some, or would you prefer tea?"

The old lady nearly turned into a puddle under Ayden's warmth. She smiled. She giggled like a schoolgirl.

The corners of Mia's lips twitched. The edges of her heart twisted. She turned away and began to move through the crowd. Pitching her voice a little above the hubbub, she asked, "Does anyone know anything about a missing child?"

The tumult lowered as though someone had dropped a blanket over them.

Mia paused. "Anyone? We found a little boy on the train the other night, but his people seem to have vanished."

A chorus of denials of knowledge rose in the entryway, the fellowship room, the sanctuary. No one had seen the child or heard of anyone seeking one.

"If you do," Mia said in each room, "send them to the Goswells."

"You're staying at the Goswells', Mia Roper?" A vaguely familiar female voice rang through the church.

Mia spun on her heel, her wide merino skirt belling out around her. "Genevieve Perry?"

"Genevieve Perry Baker now." The smiling, petite redhead threw her arms around Mia, portfolio and pencil and all. "I never thought I'd see you again."

"I never thought I'd be here again." Mia kissed the other woman's cheek. "You look beautiful. Is marriage to Jonathan Baker suiting you, then?"

"Quite, quite well. And you? No fiancé or even husband back there in the East?"

"No time for love." Mia stared at the muddy, water-stained floor. "I work too much and travel."

"How exciting. Did you come in on one of the trains?"

"I did." Mia nodded to her left wrist. "A relatively minor injury, but a nuisance."

"A rather painful nuisance, I should think." Genevieve's vivid-green eyes narrowed, and her lips bowed. "Is there any significance to you staying with the Goswells?"

"Nothing beyond the idea that God may have a rather unpleasant sense of humor, though I suppose that's blasphemous to say in a church."

"Or anywhere." Genevieve tucked her arm through Mia's and began to shepherd her toward the front door. "You must come to our house for coffee and catch me up on everything. Catch *us* up on everything, to be more precise. A dozen of us are making gallons of soup and pounds of bread rolls for these people's lunch."

Mia smiled at her friend from the years she spent teaching school before receiving the opportunity for journalism work in the East. "Not today. I have work to do." The instant the words emerged, an ache opened in her chest, a chasm in which lodged a cold, hard boulder into which she had long ago tucked all her wishes for friendship, family, and a home. "I'm only here on assignment."

"Ah, your journalism career." Genevieve sighed. "I thought maybe you were here to renew . . ." Her gaze strayed across the room to where Ayden poured coffee for a line of men and women.

Mia flicked her attention to Charmaine, who was still positioned against the front wall like an ornamental bit of statuary. "That's over and has been for a year and a half." Her voice was cold, her heart frozen enough to hurt.

"Ah, the perfect Charmaine. If she weren't so kind, we'd all hate her."

"I don't see what's kind about standing by the door instead of helping." Mia's tone held an edge of asperity.

Genevieve laughed. "Methinks you have a few claws still extended in that direction." She slanted a look toward Ayden.

"Not in the least. I only accepted the Goswells' invitation to stay with them so others could use my room at the boardinghouse. But I have no intention of renewing any sort of relationship with Ayden Goswell." She gestured around the room with the point of her pencil. "If this hadn't happened, I would have avoided him."

"Avoided someone in Hillsdale?" Genevieve hugged Mia's arm to her rather plump side, where once she had been slight.

Mia gave her once-upon-a-time friend a narrow-eyed glance. No, Genevieve had not gained a great deal of weight, at least not the kind that would stay. Genevieve disguised her expectant motherhood beneath the shielding layers of a woolen gown, bulky coat, and over-sized scarf.

"Congratulations." Mia's throat tightened. "I thought you were going to continue to teach school."

"I was. I did. I find I prefer domesticity, though I do still tutor for the college." Genevieve grinned. "Can't let that education go to waste, as all the detractors of educating women say it will. Think how intelligent my children will be."

"Your children would be intelligent even if you'd never taken a class." Mia glanced around the room again, wondering if she could leave by the church's other door. She didn't want to walk past the beauteous Miss Finney to leave.

Not that she knew where to go next. She could go out to the wreck, but she didn't want to walk all that way in the snow. Walking to the wreck alone was not a good idea. Ayden had been her escort. He, how-ever, had relinquished his coffee-serving duties to the wife of a science professor, a woman known for her generosity in feeding students. He was heading straight for Charmaine Finney, whose face lit up at his approach.

Mia turned her attention to Genevieve. "I think I would like to go to your house after all, if I may, if the invitation is still open."

"It is." Genevieve winked. "We'll slip out the back. Our house is almost directly behind the church."

Genevieve led Mia through the sanctuary to a narrow side door. Beyond it, a flight of steps led down to another door. The instant the first door closed behind them, the din inside the church diminished to a dull roar. Beyond the second door, the snow-clad world enveloped them in a calming hush.

"That's better." Genevieve's footfalls crunched on the ground. "Now tell me what you're doing back here if not to see the Goswells and why you haven't written to any of us even to tell us you were coming and what have you been doing with yourself—"

"Enough." Mia laughed. "One question at a time." She kicked her feet through the powdery surface snow. "I'm here on assignment for the magazine I write for. If the editor likes my article, she'll hire me as a full-time reporter."

"That's exciting. Have you been writing all along, though?" Genevieve unlatched the gate in a fence across the lane.

"I have. Quite a lot between periodicals in Boston and New York and even one article in a Philadelphia magazine."

"*Godey's?*" Genevieve's eyes sparkled with excitement.

Mia shook her head. "I haven't been that blessed yet. But this new magazine might end up even better than *Godey's*. We want to show women they can make other choices in their lives than being wives and mothers and to consider that before they think marriage is their only option."

Genevieve closed the gate behind them with a decisive click. "Being a wife and mother is a noble calling for a lady. Just as noble as being a teacher or a doctor or a telegraph operator."

"Well, of course, but some of us . . ." Mia trailed off.

Her gaze fixed on Genevieve's house, which had smoke curling from chimneys into the blue-white sky, dispersing the aroma of roasting meat. Yellow gingham curtains hung in ruffles from the kitchen windows. At one side of the door, a trellis promised a bower of fragrant climbing roses in the summer, and lace draperies graced the windows of what was likely a parlor.

"I know this house." Her voice emerged as a mere whisper. "It's across the street from the Blamey house."

"It is. Sadly, Professor Blamey retired and moved himself and his wife to Pittsburgh to be closer to their children." Genevieve started up the steps of the back porch but hesitated before opening the kitchen door. "No one lives there now, but there's talk Ayden Goswell intends to buy it for when—that is, if—he and Charmaine marry."

"That," Mia said between her teeth, "would be foolish."

Ayden had proposed to her in the rear garden of that house during a summer barbecue. They had settled in a gazebo as the sun dipped below the horizon. With all the courtliness of the medieval knights he studied, he had dropped to one knee and pledged his undying love no matter what life tossed their way.

He had lied.

Mia feared she whimpered like a wounded puppy.

Genevieve gave her a one-armed hug. "It's just talk. You know how this town is about gossip." She yanked open the back door.

Warmth greeted them like a mother's embrace. With the enthusiasm of a flock of birds settling in a tree at dusk, the chatter of female voices rose and fell in rapid-fire conversation. In seconds, Mia was surrounded by former colleagues, new female students, and a handful of women stranded in town by the train wreck. They hugged her. They fussed over her bandaged wrist; they scolded her for leaving them behind without a word of where she'd gone or what she was doing.

"You could have died in that city, and none of us would have been the wiser," said a former classmate who now worked at the bank.

Mia's legs wobbled. Her eyes blurred. "A few people knew where I was."

"Like Ayden Goswell," someone called from the far side of the large kitchen.

"Yes, Ayden knew." Someone in front of her rose and pushed her chair toward Mia. "Sit down. You look like you're ready to fall down."

"You should have stayed in bed." Genevieve poured a cup of coffee and set it before Mia.

"I have work to do." Mia wrapped her hands around the cup to warm them. "There's a child at the Goswells' whose mother has gone missing."

She explained about the little boy and the woman who disappeared from the train in the chaos. The ladies exclaimed, offering their prayers for the mother to be found. While carrots and potatoes were peeled, onions chopped, and stock stirred, the talk turned to Ayden and his work at the college, then diverted to the wreck. Genevieve, always good at arithmetic, pulled up a slate and chalk and began to ask for suggestions on how to provide people with enough food and shelter.

"We have finite supplies until the tracks are cleared," she reminded them all.

The ladies took turns listing what supplies they had on hand, and Genevieve tallied up pounds of flour, sugar, and root vegetables. Before she finished, someone once again demanded to know why Mia had written to no one.

Mia gazed at the sea of faces around her—her college classmates, some friends from the years she lived with her now-deceased aunt in Hillsdale, some from her teaching days. She remembered the camaraderie and frustrations of life they'd shared and found no useful response. "I think I was just ready to put Hillsdale behind me. I wanted to forget—"

The back door opened with a blast of frosty air. The women fell silent, all gazes flashing to the newcomer—except Mia's. Some scent, some indefinable perception of mind or perhaps the prompting of her heart, told her who had arrived.

"I'm sorry to interrupt, ladies, and I'm looking for Mia Rope—ah, there you are." Ayden strode forward and rested his hand on her shoulder. "You disappeared on me."

"You were occupied." Mia didn't look at him. His touch was enough to disconcert her without adding the sight of him to the mixture of chills from the blast of cold wind from the open door and an internal ice pick working at her heart.

"Momentarily only. I'm ready to head out to the wreck now. If you want to go with an escort, you'll have to say good-bye to the present company."

Mia glanced around at the circle of open, friendly, and now-familiar faces—sisters in scholarship, potential good friends—and an impression like an anchor cable urged her to stay.

"Charmaine," someone murmured.

She understood the mention of the lady. She had laid claim to Ayden, and he couldn't risk alienating her and thus her father.

As for Mia's career, its needs admonished her to get up and go with him. She might lose the opportunity for another part of her train wreck story. But her heart warned her to stay where she was, warm, safe, still free of caring too deeply for Ayden—when she managed to not be near him. But two good stories would guarantee her a permanent position with the journal. Perhaps even three, when she had enough to write about the rescued child whose people seemed to have disappeared.

She shrugged Ayden's hand off her shoulder and rose. "I'll come back, if I may."

"You are always welcome here." Genevieve hugged her and murmured in her ear. "You should stay."

Genevieve had said something similar a year and a half ago as well. But Mia had gone, and Ayden hadn't waited all that long before taking up the courtship of Charmaine Finney. Choosing her career had been the right choice then. It was the right choice now. Her heart had survived the wound Ayden had dealt it in '54; it could survive another hour or two in his company.

Chapter Six

She looked like the old Mia, sitting there amid a crowd of ladies, laughing, voice sparkling, hands moving as though she illustrated her words in the air despite her bandaged wrist. She belonged with these women. They were so intelligent and kind, committed to their families and committed to education. Many times, he had seen Mia in such a group, peeling potatoes or knitting while discussing Hannibal crossing the Alps on elephants or Plato or something else of an intellectual pursuit.

For a moment, when he had stood there with his hand on her shoulder as though he had a right to touch her, let alone act so possessively, he had wanted to pull his hair and cry out, "Why couldn't you see that this is the best place in the world to live?"

Because she longed to be a journalist and Hillsdale possessed only the *Standard*, the smallest of newspapers, let alone a magazine that would print the sort of long pieces at which she excelled.

"I fetched the sleigh." He spoke with a curtness he didn't bother to disguise. "I can't keep the horses standing any longer."

"Ooh, a ride in the sleigh," several of the ladies chorused.

"A far cry from when we were students and not allowed to ride in a vehicle with just a gentleman." Genevieve winked. "And of course the two of you never broke that rule."

Mia blushed and laughed, then gathered up her pocketbook and portfolio and rose. "It's been lovely to see all of you again. Perhaps—do you all think I could interview some of you for my article about women in academia with men?"

"Come back any day." Genevieve nudged her toward the door. "We'll be meeting daily to cook, I expect, as long as the town is full of all these passengers."

"Now that you mention passengers . . ." Mia crossed the room to where two women who looked like governesses sat in a corner shelling peas. The voices of the others drowned out Mia's words, but the ladies nodded, their eyes cast down. No doubt more victims for her journalistic pen.

"Mia." His tone was sharp. "I'm leaving."

The last two words she had spoken to him until she stood poised in the doorway to the train: "I don't care if you've reneged on your promise, Ayden Goswell. I'm leaving." And she had.

Because she hadn't loved him enough to stay. She accused him of not loving her enough to go. Perhaps they were both right.

He yanked open the kitchen door, nodded good-bye to the ladies, and set his mouth in a firm line, while Mia shared a few more embraces with her old friends and exited the house ahead of him.

"How did you know I was here?" she asked.

"I saw you leave with Genevieve." He slipped his hand beneath her elbow. "Careful. It's slippery where people have walked."

"I'm surprised you noticed anything but Miss Finney." She opened the gate before he could do the gentlemanly honors. "She looked so picturesque, standing there by the door, out of the way of the hoi polloi."

"That is unkind." Ayden closed the gate with too much vigor, sending the crash reverberating through the neighborhood like a cannon blast. "And unfair. She had just brought a basket of pastries for those stranded."

"Produced in her tidy little kitchen, away from the hoi polloi." With a half smile tossed in his direction, Mia stepped into the sleigh. "Or should I say riffraff?"

Ayden yanked the reins from the hitching post. "When did you turn so mean?"

"When I had to survive in the city on my own." She looked away from him so her hood hid her face.

A twinge of guilt poked at Ayden, and from that stemmed annoyance. "Do not blame that on me, Euphemia Roper. No one made you go."

"And no one made you stay."

"You have an answer for everything, do you not?" He climbed into the sleigh and gathered the reins.

"I get paid to answer questions." Mia moved as far away from him as the seat allowed. Half a dozen inches lay between them. Her portfolio leaned against her side, a pen warrior's shield to fend him off.

For a moment, Ayden was tempted to toss the scuffed leather case into Genevieve's yard. But Mia would simply leap out and retrieve it.

Instead, he reached behind him and gathered up two fur rugs. "You will want to cover up with one of these."

"Thank you." She took the rug from him without looking in his direction.

As he covered himself with the fur as best he could while still holding the reins, he remembered the last time they'd ridden in a sleigh together. They had staved off the cold by sitting close beneath the same rug. For once, the portfolio had not lain between them. They had touched from shoulder to thigh, their gloved fingers entwined—

He yanked his thoughts from that direction and gestured to her wrap with the reins. "You might want to pull that all the way up to your neck. The wind will be stronger out of town."

"I can't seem to manage it with just the one hand." She held up her left hand. "My fingers don't want to grip very well."

"Should I help you?" He looked at her, and their eyes met, held for just a moment too long.

She licked her lips and broke the contact. "No, thank you. I won't feel the cold."

With Euphemia Roper beside him, neither would he. Her nearness always managed to heat his blood, whether from ire or yearning. Ire, or at least annoyance, was the name of the game today. She no longer made him long to touch her.

He could believe that if he did not look at her or stand close enough to inhale her scent or . . .

He flicked the reins with more vigor than necessary. The horses plunged forward, the bells on their harness jingling in discordant chorus. Their hooves rang on the hard-packed snow. Hissing like wind through leaves, the sleigh runners followed in the ruts of other vehicles before them. Beyond the sounds of the horses and sleigh, the world lay silent. No one wanted to be out in the cold unless necessary, and at that hour, most had tucked themselves by fires to eat lunch.

Between Mia and Ayden, the silence stretched to the edge of town. It expanded beyond the outskirts and into the surrounding farmland. The lack of conversation between them, when once they only ceased talking to embrace, grew so profound after the first quarter mile Ayden's ears began to ring as though the harness bells had attached themselves to his hat.

"Did you get snow like this in Boston this year?" he asked out of desperation.

"Nothing that lasted like it does here."

"I found the ocean wind harsh."

"The bay and cape protect us a good bit, but I think nor'easters . . ." She stopped and a plume of white vapor swirled in front of her face.

"Ayden Goswell, when were we ever reduced to talking about the weather?"

He fixed his gaze on the sleek gray horses. "Since you got aboard an eastbound train and swore you would never return."

"And you chose not to follow me."

"This is my home. I had a chance to stay here and help my father."

"And I, of course, never having had the luxury of a real home, found going to more lucrative pastures wiser."

"You could have had a permanent home here."

"And we could have built a permanent home and professorship with me in Boston instead of the temporary position you have now."

"The position in Boston might have been temporary, you know that now as well as you knew it then."

"But wait," she continued as though he hadn't spoken, sarcasm creeping into her tone. "You will have a permanent position for the mere cost of a wedding ring through your nose."

Ayden reined in so fast the sleigh slewed sideways, and Mia's portfolio fell against him. He shoved it upright as he turned to glare at her. "Explain right now what you mean by that."

She smiled, but it didn't reach her eyes. They were chips of green ice. "You're the most eligible bachelor in Hillsdale. You marry Miss Charmaine Finney, and her daddy ensures you get the professorship, now that it's a permanent one. Then Daddy gets to order you around the rest of your life."

"Who told you that?" Ayden spoke between clenched teeth to keep himself from shouting.

Mia shrugged too slowly, too dismissively. "Your sister."

"I should have known."

"And Genevieve."

His stomach sank. "What does she know of it?"

"And Rose and Marianne and—"

"Enough." He flung his hands up as though warding off blows.

The revelation of such gossip hurt like fists to the gut.

The horses began to move, flinging Ayden against the side of the sleigh. His head struck the seatback with a resounding crack, and he remained motionless as the spots before his eyes ceased dancing on the snow, letting the horses have their heads.

"Are you all right?" Mia took the reins from his slack hands and drew the team to a halt. "Ayden, are you hurt? That bump sounded nasty." She leaned toward him, her face mere inches from his.

"I'm all right. Just stunned." He concentrated on ensuring the horses pulled straight and even through the runner ruts in the snow alongside the railroad tracks. "Rosalie might not survive my wrath if she persists in talking about my courtship of Miss Finney that way."

"I told you that it isn't just Rosalie. It seems to be the prevailing belief amongst the ladies of this town."

"She started it and eggs them on." Ayden emitted a grumble of annoyance through his teeth. "She's just angry because I don't like her beau."

"Why not?"

"He's an uneducated lout who talked her out of going to school." Ayden glowered at the first glimpse of the wreck by daylight.

Beside him, Mia stiffened and cradled her left wrist against her middle. "Getting on another train is going to be difficult."

"A pity you didn't find it so a year and a half ago," Ayden muttered.

"A pity you couldn't keep your word." She blinked as though clearing her eyes of tears, but her voice remained impassive.

Ayden squeezed his eyes shut against the lack of pain on her lovely face. "I never broke my word about wanting to make you my wife. I simply changed my mind about where I would teach after Pa had his accident."

"He seems quite all right now."

"He is, but he wasn't two years ago. A man needs a good, strong back to run his hardware store."

"And Dr. Goswell thinks he can move from swords to plowshares?"

Ayden grinned in appreciation of her wit. "Very nice, Mia, mi am—" He stopped before using the pet name he'd used so effortlessly before. Mia, mi amore. Mia, my love.

"I was never your love." Mia sounded weary now. "You would have come with me if I had been."

"You could have stayed."

"And done what here in Hillsdale? Write a gossip column for the *Standard*?" She jerked her face away, but her hand shot up as though she wiped away tears. "It wasn't the best writing job in Boston, but it was a writing job, and you had that teaching position waiting. We'd have done well together."

"So do you still have that position?" His question was more a taunt than a query. Mom had subscribed to the periodical that hired Mia. Not six months after she left, her name ceased appearing under contributors.

Beside him, her lips tightened. "They encountered financial difficulties and let me go, but the editor recommended me to her colleagues, and I have always had writing work."

"I still have my teaching position."

"Will they hire you?"

"I believe they will."

"Would they hire you permanently if you were not with Charmaine?"

Ayden flinched but tried to lighten the tension between them. "You apparently remember how to fence with your tongue, even if you have forgotten how to fence with rapiers."

"I have not forgotten how to fence with rapiers."

He had taught her the ancient art, and she had been an apt pupil. They had spent many enjoyable hours sparring during his holidays home from the East.

"We should—" He stopped himself. No, they should not have a fencing match. In their present state, they just might remove the buttons from the ends of the rapiers and stab one another with more than their tongues. "We should stop sniping at one another," he finished instead.

"Because you do not wish to answer my question?" She slid him a sidelong glance, a mocking smile.

He stiffened. "My qualifications to teach classics at the college have nothing to do with my courtship of the department director's daughter."

"I know that, Dr. Goswell." Her tone was too sweet. "But surely many others have applied who are as much as or more qualified."

"A direct hit under my guard." He rubbed his head where he had smacked it on the seatback. The flesh was tender, perhaps forming a lump. His head did not feel as bruised as did his spirit, his heart.

He took a deep breath to keep his voice steady. "I began to court Charmaine before a permanent opening at the college was announced."

"Of course you did." She patted his arm. "And if she throws you over for someone else, you can always go away to find work."

Ayden caught hold of her hand before she could draw it back. "Mia, stop it. It is not in your nature to be mean-spirited."

"I didn't think it was in your nature to be untrustworthy." She blinked and turned her face away but squeezed his fingers for a fraction of a second before tugging her hand free and rolling it into the edge of the blanket. "We will simply not talk about our past together or about your future at the college."

"That seems safe."

And useless.

"Shall I tell you about an ancient parchment one of the other professors brought back from the Middle East?"

"You haven't seen it yet." She leaned forward to study the train wreckage. "I overheard your conversation on the pavement this morning."

"I am sorry about that." Ayden concentrated on guiding the horses through drifted snow, though instinct made him wish to touch Mia's hand or arm or smooth cheek. "Finney has become insufferable since he became director of the Classics Department."

"He was never a kind man."

"But he liked you."

"He liked my work until he learned you were courting me." She hugged her portfolio against her side and gazed at the rug on her lap. "He never thought me good enough for you."

Ayden hesitated, choosing his words with care to inject the right amount of jocularity into his tone. "I and my family thought I was good enough, and so did all your friends. What does it matter what a curmudgeon like that thinks?"

"A great deal when it comes to your career." Green eyes flashed up at him. "But you knew that, did you not, when you chose to let me go east alone?"

"Mia, I thought we agreed—"

"Your father was nearly himself by the time we were to leave." She raised her voice over his protest. "He could have hired someone to help. He said so himself."

"Mia, stop it." He reined in and forked his fingers into his hair as though he needed to keep his head from exploding. "We agreed to let this go."

"It seems I cannot." Her gloved fingers were creating half-moon indentations in the soft leather of her portfolio. "I should not have come with you today."

"You should not have gone without me a year and a half ago." If she wanted to have this out, then they would. "If anyone made the wrong decision, it was you. You could have found the individual work like you do now if you'd stayed here."

"Not without the connections I have now. I had to go to Boston to have a chance at a real career in letters. But you chose not to understand that."

"I understand that having a career is more important to you than I was."

And after she'd gotten on that train, he had walked deep into the woods and cried like a child who had just lost his family. Even now, the memory of that day tightened his chest and brought moisture to his eyes—or perhaps the moisture came from the chill of the wind and not remembered anguish.

For a year, as he saw how strong his father was, how easily he could have hired someone to perform the tasks requiring heavy labor at the store, Ayden questioned the rightness of his decision. Then he met Charmaine, beautiful and somehow sad to be in Hillsdale instead of Philadelphia, a sadness he put down to the recent loss of her mother and her friends back East, and he thought perhaps he could forget about Mia.

"You could have stayed a little longer—long enough to give us time to work out our differences." He spoke so softly he wasn't certain she heard.

She sighed with a gust that sent a stream of vapor into the gray afternoon. "Of course I could stay here no longer. I had already taken money for an assignment in Boston." She lifted a handkerchief to her nose.

"And I'd already turned down the Boston position and accepted the one here." He spoke through a constricted throat.

"You made a major decision without consulting me." Her voice remained calm, but beneath the handkerchief, her lower lip quivered ever so slightly.

He raised his hand, reached out, stopped himself from smoothing her mouth steady just in time.

She turned her face away. "I was expected to break my word and likely never have my own dreams fulfilled."

"You could have fulfilled your dreams in other ways. That work was only—"

Mia's hand clamped on his arm. "Do. Not. Say. It." She released him as though his sleeve had turned into a flaming torch. "It wasn't great work, but it was a start in the right direction. It's gotten me further, whether you like it or not. And like it or not, we need to work together to find this child's people."

"And arguing here or in front of anyone will not do anyone any good." He relaxed against the sleigh seat and began to look for railroad workers moving around the train. "I'd do anything not to upset my parents especially."

"So would I. They were the closest thing to parents I ever had."

For a moment, her indifferent mask slipped, revealing the sad, vulnerable girl who had moved to Hillsdale twelve years earlier to live with an aging relative who had never had children and did not, apparently, want them. She gave Mia shelter, the occasional meal when she thought of it, and nothing else. Mia didn't seem to mind all that much. She had known little else in a vagabond life of being shunted from one relative after another, moving on to the next one when the previous one died.

Unwittingly, however, the great-aunt in Hillsdale had given Mia one great gift—a house full of books. Mia had begun a systematic reading of those tomes.

Ayden's gaze strayed to a now snow-clad hill on the far side of the railroad tracks where he had met Mia. She'd been sprawled on the grass with a book open before her. Her dress was so worn and faded its original color was impossible to guess, and the skirt was far too short for modesty. Her hair hung in tangles around her face, her skin was too brown for accepted beauty, but she looked him straight in the eye with those stunning, slanted green eyes, and said, "You're Ayden Goswell, home from school in Boston. You can help me work out this bit in Greek that's giving me trouble."

She had taught herself ancient Greek because she had read all the English-language books in her great-aunt's house.

Bowled over, Ayden had helped her with the translation, and they discussed Ptolemy's theories of geography and astronomy for two hours. When the sun began to set, she sprang to her feet, panic etching her features, and sprinted away, her worn skirt sailing around her bare calves.

Ayden went home and told his parents they needed to find some way to get her an education. In three months, Mia was in college, and Ayden was in love.

He shook his head in an effort to clear it of memories and spotted a group of men in railway uniforms raking through the burned remains of a mail car. Before he reined in, Mia scrambled over the side of the sleigh and plowed across the field of snow trampled by people and vehicles from the night of the wreck.

"Sirs? Hello there, can you help us?" She waved her pencil in the air like a flag.

Ayden climbed down with more dignity. "We're in search of some information," he called.

The men glanced back and glared at them. "We aren't giving out information any more'n we already have."

"No, no, not about the wreck." Mia gave the men a smile warm enough to melt a path through the snow. "Of course we'd all like to know what went wrong, and I know accidents happen, especially on stormy nights. But what we want to know is how we can reunite a little boy and his momma. They seem to have been separated from one another after the crash. Can you help?"

"Not likely," one of the men growled.

"No? You look like you can." She tilted her head and opened her eyes wide.

She was going to bat her long lashes any moment now.

Ayden didn't know if he should laugh or toss her over his shoulder and haul her away before she gave these men the wrong idea about her character.

He moved closer to her, rested a possessive hand on her shoulder, and addressed the men. "The little boy was wandering down the aisle when the train wrecked. Miss Roper here picked him up—"

"I was thinking perhaps a passenger list would help?" She interrupted with brute force, casting him a quelling glance.

"If you want a passenger list, you'll have to get it from headquarters." The spokesman turned back to the burned-out car.

"And where is that?" Mia asked.

"Jackson." The men returned their attention to the mangled wreckage.

Mia kicked a clump of frozen snow. "Even if we send a telegram, the answer could take days to get back to us."

One of the railroad workers sneered at her. "Yeah, 'cause the mail ain't gettin' through."

"Precisely. Which is why I am asking you gentlemen for aid." Her smile did not falter.

The men glared.

Ayden laid his hand on her arm and scanned his gaze along the line of twisted, tilted, and surprisingly undamaged cars. "Do you want to risk looking in your car?"

"You'd do that with me?" She glanced up at him with her eyes gleaming and the first warm smile she'd granted him.

He'd do about anything for her at that moment.

They thanked the railroad men, who ignored them, then drove along the train.

Mia half turned on the sleigh seat to gaze at the wreckage. Some cars had burned when the boilers in the engine exploded. Some lay on their sides. Others tilted like weary men leaning against an invisible wall. Most, however, stood upright, as though all they needed were engines to haul them on down the line to their destination. But those mangled and burned cars toward the front sent the hairs on Ayden's arms prickling.

A shudder ran through Mia powerful enough to shake the sleigh seat. "And I was annoyed I could only get a seat in a rear car. If I'd been closer to the front—" She hugged her arms across her middle.

Ayden slipped his arm around her. He intended it for comfort. The impact of feeling her narrow shoulders in the circle of his arm was like he'd just slammed face-first into that invisible wall. His arm shook with his wanting to draw her closer for comfort and for a way to erase the past hurt between them.

But Mia shrugged her shoulders and slipped from beneath his hold. "I believe," she said without looking at him, "you gave up the right to touch me in August of fifty-four." Then she leaped from the sleigh, sliding a bit on the frozen top crust of the snow, and sped toward the train. "Sir, sir, wait."

Ayden hadn't noticed the man in a railway uniform until Mia called to him. He paused in the doorway of one of the tilted cars. Unlike the other workers, who were armed with relatively harmless rakes and picks, this man carried a gun on his hip.

Chapter Seven

⚜

At sight of the man's gun, Mia slid to a stop, clutching her port-folio to her chest like a shield. If she hadn't been holding the notebook, she would have raised her hands in a gesture of surrender.

The railroad man dropped his hand—to the butt of his gun. "What do you folks want?"

Mia summoned her best smile. "We came to look for something in the car in which I was—"

The man cut her off with a brusque shake of his head. "No, ma'am. No one goes in the cars until they've all been searched. We won't have looting on my watch."

"We aren't looters," Mia and Ayden protested together.

Snow crunched behind Mia, and the man drew his gun from its holster. "Stay where you are, sir."

"I'm Ayden Goswell, history professor at the college." Ayden's voice was tight and too far behind Mia for her comfort.

She slid one foot back. "And I'm Euphemia Roper, a reporter for—"

"The professor I might believe, but a lady reporter?" The man threw back his head and laughed. The gun wavered. "You'll have to come up with something better than that one, missy, if you want me to let you in any of the cars. Now get going back the way you came."

"This has to do with a lost child," Mia tried again. "We're trying to find . . . his . . . people. I found him wandering—"

The gun ceased wavering. The muzzle, surely as wide as a blunderbuss barrel, was pointed directly at her chest. "Get out of here, or I will—"

Snow crunched like a hundred eggshells underfoot, and Ayden's arms closed around her, dragging her backward, down beneath the bullet whining overhead like a bee out of season.

Her head on her drawn-up knees, Mia trembled and gasped and gabbled nonsense exclamations and a few prayers. Ayden crouched beside her, his hand on her head, murmuring soothing, incomprehensible words of comfort. And all the while, the echo of the shot reverberated across the snow-laden landscape and gentle hills.

"He's gone now." Ayden grasped Mia's arms and lifted her to her feet. "And we should be as well."

"To the sheriff, I expect." While Ayden sprinted to the horses' heads, Mia stumbled to the sleigh and collapsed onto the seat.

It rocked with the agitation of horses too well trained and old to have bolted but still restive in their traces. Mia's stomach shifted in the opposite direction, and if she'd eaten any breakfast or lunch, she would have been sick right there in front of Ayden. She scooped up a handful of clean, white snow and held it to her brow. "What was that all about? Shooting looters on sight?"

"Possibly, but we weren't looting. And he didn't fire until you mentioned the child." The horses calmed, and Ayden returned to the sleigh. "I don't think he actually shot at us."

"He aimed at me." Mia faced him on the narrow seat.

At one time, he was too close and too far away. If he had slipped an arm around her then, she would have succumbed to the longing to be held and rested her head on his shoulder, where she could hear the strong, even rhythm of his heart and inhale his fresh, clean scent from exposure to the winter air. But with them, closeness too easily led to cuddling, and cuddling led to kissing, and only a courting couple intending to wed had a right to that sort of nearness. She couldn't even hold his hand.

In that moment, with Ayden mere inches away, Mia missed him more than she had when she was nearly a thousand miles away. They hadn't just lost their future together; they had lost their friendship from the past.

Her eyes burned. Her lips quivered. She pressed her snowy glove to her mouth and closed her eyes to hold in the tears.

"Let's get to the sheriff." Ayden's voice was rough.

Mia tucked herself into the far corner of the sleigh and drew the lap rug to her chin despite the pain doing so brought to her left wrist. "Perhaps we should stop and tell the other workers or ask them if they know who he is."

"If he's from the railroad, I'll be surprised." Ayden's jaw looked as hard as the railroad ties. "Even a train guard wouldn't shoot without cause."

"Most criminals don't shoot without cause."

Ayden cast her a sharp glance through a veil of newly falling snow. "How would you know that?"

"I've done some reporting on crime."

"Mia, how could you? That's dangerous."

"It can also pay well." She looked past him as he turned the sleigh back the way they'd come. "The men aren't there any longer."

The burned mail car where they had been raking through the debris now lay abandoned beneath the dusting of fresh snow—snow filling in footprints around the tracks and cars.

"Frightened off, like us?" Mia asked.

"Or counterfeit train workers, like the man with the gun." Ayden clucked to the horses and snapped the reins, encouraging them to increase their pace. "I'll take you home, then go on to the sheriff."

Mia stiffened. "You will do no such thing. I'm as much a witness to what happened as you are."

"Yes, but the sheriff won't take you as seriously."

"Oh, will he not?" Mia clenched her fists and gasped as pain shot through her left wrist. "Are you telling me that even with the college here with brilliant female students, the law officers do not take the word of a woman as seriously as the word of a man?"

"The women don't vote."

"Which also needs to be rectified. Do you know that New Jersey's original constitution gave women the right to vote if they owned—stop laughing at me, Ayden Benaiah Goswell. I am completely serious. The only bad thing that came out of it was that some men realized the error and changed the wording to say that only *men* owning property could vote."

"I know. I know." Ayden wiped snow and mirth tears from his lashes. "I was the one who shared that tidbit of history with you."

"Of course you did. I forgot."

"I'm surprised. You don't seem to forget anything."

"Not as much as I'd like to forget."

Such as how his deep-blue eyes sparkled like faceted sapphires when he laughed. Such as the richness of that laughter. Such as how much she loved the sound of his voice.

"You seem to have forgotten about me well enough." Ayden stepped from the sleigh to guide the horses around in the tight ruts buried beneath drifted snow.

Mia watched him, flicking glances toward the train for the man with the gun, then back to Ayden. He was too tall, too broad a target for her to feel secure about him walking in front of the team.

He was also too tall, too broad to look like a professor of classics, history, Latin, and Greek. He was too handsome by far to resemble what people thought of scholars. He resembled a man who hauled freight or rescued maidens in distress.

He had rescued her from a life of poverty and potential crime. He had recognized her as more than that ragged Roper girl simply because she had been reading Greek when he encountered her.

"I have forgotten most of the Greek I knew." The remark was inane. She wasn't even certain he heard it as he strode back to the sleigh and slid in beside her.

"You probably haven't had much cause to use Greek." He gathered the reins and clucked to the horses.

They headed off along the tracks. Ayden and Mia stared at the train. They saw no one.

"Do you remember your Italian?" Ayden asked.

Mia relaxed with the change in topic and the passing of the wreck behind them. "I refreshed my knowledge when I wrote an article about a lady's fencing club a few months ago."

"I would like to see one of those here." Ayden urged the team to greater speed. "If you stayed around here, you could start one."

"Fencing with ladies was boring after—" She slapped her fingers across her mouth, but the damage was done.

Ayden flashed her a grin. "After fencing with me?"

She said nothing.

"Are you sure you don't want a match?"

"Dr. Finney wouldn't like it."

But she would. Suddenly, she wanted to do nothing more than to clash blades with Ayden.

"Dr. Finney does not rule my life." Ayden's hands jerked, and the horses sped up.

They swung onto Broad Street at a faster clip than necessary. The sleigh rocked onto one runner, and someone shouted at him to have a care.

He didn't. He kept up the pace until they reached the sheriff's office. In front of the door, he leaped out and hitched the horses, then rounded the sleigh to assist Mia to the pavement.

"I warned you how they'll view your word in here, so mind your tongue. I don't want you arrested for assaulting an officer with that blade you sheathe behind your teeth."

Mia laughed. She couldn't help herself. The gurgle of amusement rose from her chest and burbled from her lips. And with it, the rocky shell she'd built to protect her heart cracked just enough for her to see how much she had loved this man, how much she could still love him.

She tried to stuff a wad of angry memories into the breach to keep the tender feelings safely inside. "I'll be good, Professor Goswell."

"All right." He offered her his arm and led her into the office.

Heat and the odors of wet wool, old coffee, and bodies not as clean as they should be filled the room. Half a dozen people steamed around the stove, and a vaguely familiar-looking young man with curly red hair and tired blue eyes stood behind a tall desk.

Ayden's arm stiffened beneath Mia's hand. "At least he's here and not at my house," he grumbled.

The deputy glanced their way. "What do you want, Goswell? If it's about your sister—"

"It's official business," Ayden said.

"I see that." The deputy looked at Mia, and a jolt of recognition shot through her. "Did you catch her stealing again?"

The chatter around the stove ceased.

Mia flinched and yanked her hand from Ayden's arm. She gripped her portfolio with both hands as though it were a lifeline keeping her from sliding off a tilting deck. Or, in this case, racing out the door. "I never stole a thing worth more than a penny or two, Deputy Lambert."

"I think I'm missing something here." Ayden stared from one of them to the other. "You know Fletcher Lambert?"

"Fletcher? He's Rosalie's Fletcher?" Mia felt light-headed. "I didn't know his Christian name, but we had the misfortune of meeting about ten years ago."

Lambert grinned. "She was my first arrest. Caught her stealing pencils from the stationer's shop."

"You arrested her over a pencil?" Ayden gritted his teeth. "That does it, you know, Lambert. A man that unkind doesn't deserve my sister."

"He was only doing his duty." Mia cast her gaze at the mud-streaked floor tiles. "I was wrong to take anything. I took pencils and paper from wherever I could." Her cheeks burned. "I have paid their owners all back since."

"But you never told me."

Mia pressed her cold, damp gloves to her hot cheeks. "I didn't want you to think ill of me."

"I wouldn't have—" Ayden glanced at the people near the stove, then back to Lambert. "Never mind that now. We need to talk to the sheriff."

"He's not here. I'm the only one on station duty."

"Then may we write out a report for you to give to the sheriff?" Ayden spoke with exaggerated patience.

"Of course." Lambert removed paper, ink, and pens from behind his desk. "Do you want to tell it to me, or do you want to write it out yourself? I need to know as many specific details as possible—time, place, incident, who was involved." He paused. "What are you reporting besides that lost child?"

"A shooting." Ayden smiled.

Lambert paled. "You should have said. Is anyone hurt?"

"No one is hurt," Ayden said, "but someone is impersonating a railroad worker, or perhaps four men are."

Mia and Ayden wrote out separate reports. When they finished, Deputy Lambert laid them out before him, reading first one, then the other, then the first again.

"Did the two of you plan ahead what you'd say?" He frowned at them.

They had studiously avoided talking about the incident.

"Your stories are nearly word for word the same," Lambert continued. "Very peculiar. And so is the incident. We'll send someone out there as soon as we can. Meanwhile, stay away from the train."

"It's snowing too hard to go back now." Ayden crossed the room and opened the door, allowing a blast of snow-laden wind to sweep into the station. "Mia—Miss Roper?"

Mia preceded him out the door. Ayden drew it shut behind them, but not before Lambert called, "Better get that one home before the other one yanks on the bit."

"And that one needs to keep his mouth shut if he wants to continue courting my sister." Ayden jerked the reins from the hitching post.

Mia's lips twitched. "He likes baiting you, doesn't he?"

"Yes, and I swallow the hook too easily." He waited for Mia to clamber into the sleigh, then rounded the vehicle to his side. "I wish she would look elsewhere for a beau."

"Why don't you like him? He seems conscientious about his work. And isn't he likely to be sheriff one day?"

"Probably the next election." Ayden guided the sleigh into the nearly deserted street. "And his father left him a fine house, so they will be more than comfortably off. But he encourages her to want nothing more than to be a wife and mother."

"I should think she doesn't need much encouragement along those lines. She's wonderful with the Herring children and the little boy."

"She has a fine mind she's letting go to waste."

"So where did Miss Finney attend college?" Mia gave him a sweet smile.

Ayden's jaw worked as though he ground his teeth.

"Or maybe," Mia pressed, "she doesn't have a fine mind to waste, and all she needs is a pretty face and a father in high places."

"The city," Ayden said between his teeth, "hasn't done your manners any good."

"You can't be shy and succeed as a lady in my line of work."

"Nor have a heart."

Mia stared at the portfolio lying on her lap, watching it become dusted with snow. "Nor a heart."

Ayden drew up the horses before the Goswell house. "Why did you not tell me about the pencils?"

"You mean about being a thief?" Mia's lips worked before she could say in a calm voice, "I was afraid you would end things with me if you knew. But then you ended things with me anyway, so I may as well have told you." Her face averted from him so he couldn't see her pain, she climbed from the sleigh. "I can see myself into the house."

"Mia, I never—"

Without a backward glance, she stalked up the walk to the front door. It opened before she reached it. Light and warmth and the aroma of baking apples and cinnamon blended with the sharp scent of snow.

"Go on in, child." Mrs. Goswell made a shooing motion at Mia, then turned to the street. "You won't be here for dinner, Ayden?"

Mia stepped into the warmth of the entryway before she heard Ayden's response. Whatever it was, it seemed not to please his mother, for she closed the door with more force than necessary.

"You're all over snow, Mia. Go into the parlor and dry yourself at the fire before you catch a chill."

Mia glanced through the partially open parlor door, where Mrs. Herring and Mr. Goswell played a game of Mansion of Happiness at one small table, Mr. Divine bent over some drawings at another, and Rosalie sat on the floor amid a sea of children and blocks. Laughter and the squeals of excited children shimmered in the air. Everyone's faces shone with happiness or restfulness.

Mia turned toward the steps. "I think I'll go upstairs. I'm quite worn to a thread."

"You look tired, but you can't go hide." Mrs. Goswell took her elbow and steered her down the hallway toward the kitchen. "I was going to ask Rosalie to help me, but she's doing so well with the children, I'll recruit you for the job."

"I'm not much use with only one hand."

"You can stir soup and cake batter."

So she could. Mrs. Goswell set Mia at the table with a cup of hot coffee and a bowl of yellow batter before her. "Make sure that's perfectly smooth."

It already looked perfectly smooth to Mia, but she began to stir as instructed, as she, Rosalie, and Mrs. Goswell had done so often in the past.

"So what happened today?" Mrs. Goswell bustled back to the bubbling pots on the stove.

"We had rather a lot of excitement. First we went to the church—"

"I wasn't talking about what you did." Mrs. Goswell waved a wooden spoon in the air as though erasing Mia's words from a chalkboard. "I'm talking about between you and my son."

"Nothing has changed from a year and a half ago." Mia stirred more vigorously. "His future is here in Hillsdale, and mine is back in Boston. End of story."

Mrs. Goswell slammed a lid onto a pot. "I'd rather my son go work for the railroad like his brother than marry to secure his future at the college."

"So Rosalie—" Mia released the spoon and raised her hand to her burning eyes. "She was telling the truth about why he's courting Miss Finney?"

"Not entirely. I think he holds a great deal of affection for the lady. Is that mixed?"

"Yes, ma'am. Shall I—?"

"No, I'll take care of it. You come stir this soup."

While Mrs. Goswell poured the cake batter into pans, Mia stood before the glorious warmth of the stove and stirred a pot of savory chicken soup. They worked in silence. Down the hall, the doorbell rang, and Rosalie's happy cry floated back to the kitchen.

"That'll be Fletcher." Mrs. Goswell smiled. "Don't tell her, but he's going to ask her to marry him on Valentine's Day. He's already asked her father's permission."

"It should be a good match for her. Though Ayden doesn't seem to think so."

"That boy." Mrs. Goswell knocked her spoon on the side of the metal bowl. "He seems to think every female should attend college, when some feel called to another life."

"Like playing hostess to the future head of the Classics Department." Mia's words emerged with more asperity than she intended.

Mrs. Goswell sniffed. "Hypocritical of him, isn't it? But Miss Finney is the opposite of you, which I think is the attraction. He won't have to worry about her getting notions of striking out on her own."

Mia set aside her spoon and faced Ayden's mother. "I never intended to go off on my own. I intended for him to follow me. He had an excellent teaching opportunity in Boston, and he chose to stay here for a teaching position that isn't even certain to be there at the end of the school year."

"Because of his father, you know."

"So he says. But Mr. Goswell was up and back at the hardware store before I departed. His father's fall was an excuse to stay, not a good r-r-reason." To her horror, Mia burst into tears.

"Oh, my dear girl." Mrs. Goswell enfolded Mia in her arms and held her like she was a child. "I've prayed for two years for him to come to that realization. He hated the years he was away in the East for his advanced studies. He was afraid he wouldn't succeed out there with all those people he thought were worldlier than he was, who had fathers who were politicians and who were descended from the Mayflower settlers and all. He enjoys mucking out stalls and shoveling snow, and his pa owns a hardware store."

"And I didn't want to stay in a town where the deputy sheriff still remembers me trying to steal pencils from the stationer's. I guess I'm right." Mia drew away from Mrs. Goswell's motherly arms and fumbled in her pocket for a handkerchief. "We didn't love one another enough to be honest about our fears or overcome them for the other person."

"I'd say you put your ambition before your love. I'm afraid Ayden—"

The kitchen door swung open. "I beg your pardon." Mr. Divine took a step back. "I left something in my coat pocket, but I can return later."

"No need. I should tidy myself before dinner." Mia scuttled past Mr. Divine.

As the kitchen door swung shut behind her, Mrs. Goswell said, "Ah, Mr. Divine, you just might be what we need to shake some sense into those two."

Mia wanted to eavesdrop, but she didn't want anyone else to emerge from the parlor and see her face blotched with tears. She could guess, however, what Mrs. Goswell was up to. For both their sakes, Mia decided she should warn Ayden his mother wasn't above matchmaking.

Fortunately, she didn't have to wait too long. A mere hour after supper, Mia stood in the kitchen, icing a cake for Sunday dinner, something she found she could do with one hand, when Ayden blew through the back door on a gust of icy wind, snow crystals glowing in his dark hair and his cheeks ruddy from the cold.

He halted in mid-stride at the sight of her. "I didn't know you were that domestic."

"I'm a rather good cook, Professor Goswell. Your mother taught me. And speaking of your mother"—Mia set down her knife—"I believe your mother is hatching some scheme to get us back together."

Ayden hung his coat on one of the pegs by the back door before he responded. "She'll catch cold at any attempts there. Dr. Finney asked me tonight when I plan to make Charmaine an offer."

"And what was your answer?" Mia picked up the knife to resume icing, discovered her hand shaking, and returned the blade to the table.

"Valentine's Day makes the most sense." His hands in his pockets, Ayden propped one shoulder against the wall as though he spoke to Rosalie, not the woman whose heart he had broken. "But he reminded me there's a social on the campus that day, and she'll be preoccupied with the arrangements for that and entertaining some important people at their house afterward. So I thought I'd make it official on Friday."

Chapter Eight

*O*nly once before in his life did Ayden not want to go to church. That had been the Sunday after Mia left alone for Boston. He didn't want to answer the questions about where she was, see the sympathetic faces, or potentially hear a sermon that would prick his conscience over his reasons for staying instead of keeping his word to Mia to go.

This Sunday morning, he faced the curiosity of friends, neighbors, and colleagues as to whether or not he would continue his courtship of Charmaine Finney or renew his relationship with Mia. The only way to avoid such speculation would be to suggest Mia sit with someone else instead of his family. She could. Any number of people would welcome her in their midst. But his family and his conscience wouldn't allow him to cast her off so publicly.

Mia's presence seemed to be why Dr. Finney prodded Ayden toward a commitment when he had heretofore seemed happy with the courtship. With more men coming the following week—or whenever the tracks had been cleared for train travel—to interview for the position Ayden now held on a temporary basis, he had said he would choose an appropriate time and place. Friday, while Mia was in town, seemed like a fine day, if Charmaine would be unavailable on Valentine's Day. The proposal would surely be accepted and once and for all lay to rest any rumors that he and Mia would renew their engagement. It would stop Ma from trying to bring about that renewal. It would secure his future as a professor at the college, the work he had most wanted since talk of moving Michigan Central College to his hometown began.

Ayden had returned from the Finney household with light steps through the powdery new snowfall. At last, he would have what he wanted most—his own home, established near his family and work he loved. In a few years, he would stand a good chance of becoming the head of the Classics Department. Life could not get much better.

Then he had opened the door and saw Mia calmly icing a cake at his parents' kitchen table. Her lips were pursed and her brow furrowed, as though she labored over one of her articles or essays. She glanced up at him, showing a dusting of pounded sugar on her nose, and a mist settled between his heart and the brightness of his future. His hands fisted. The urge to slam one through the plaster wall of the kitchen surged through him. He shoved his hands into his pockets and leaned against that wall for support until his breathing slowed and his heart stopped racing. Then he told Mia he intended to make Charmaine an offer by Friday.

Something in her life of being shuffled from indifferent family member to indifferent family member, then her career in a heartless city, had taught Mia to hide her feelings behind a smooth mask of indifference. She could even smile without changing that lack of interest, as she did at that moment.

"I wish you happy with your hostess. She is so ornamental and well connected I expect an education isn't important for her."

Coup de grâce delivered, she glided from the kitchen, leaving behind a half-iced cake and the fragrance of lemons.

Ayden had slammed out of the house to shovel the inch or so of new snow. Not until he returned to the warmth of the kitchen and found Ma finishing the cake icing did he realize he'd gone out without his coat.

"What did you say to her?" Ma demanded.

"I'm proposing to Charmaine on Friday." Before Ma could respond, he took the steps to his makeshift room two at a time, but he didn't find peace or rest there.

Yet one more reason not to want to go to church—he was going his own way and not taking counsel from his parents. The Bible lying on the scarred classroom table and the simple act of worship with fellow believers would surely squeeze his conscience to a screeching point.

But of course he went. He rose early to take care of the horses and scrape some ice from the walkways, then ate breakfast in the kitchen. Then he walked to church with the entire crowd from his house, happily darting ahead to corral the two Herring children out of the street.

"I'm sorry they're being so naughty." Mrs. Herring blushed. "They haven't been able to run around for days."

"We'll organize a sledding party." Ayden grabbed Roy Herring's arm before he could toss a snowball at his sister. "I expect a lot of the children are in need of a romp."

From the shrieks and squeals in front of the church, he spoke the truth. A game of snowball tag seemed to be in progress, to the hazard of those coming to the service. One snowball came flying at Ayden's head. He ducked, and Mia cried out behind him.

He turned to see her wiping the frozen crystals from her face. "I am so sorry." He reached out to pluck a chunk of snow from the fur trim of her hood, caught sight of Charmaine and her father coming up the walk, and dropped his hand. "Take my muffler." He gave her the length of red wool around his neck, then strode past her to greet the Finneys.

"Would you like an arm, Miss Roper?" Gerrett Divine asked Mia. "I'll protect you."

Ayden tensed. He should have protected her from missiles for no other reason than she was a guest in his house. But Charmaine was there, expecting him to escort her into church.

They walked behind Mia and Gerrett. The two of them chatted about something in New York City, while Ayden had no idea what Charmaine was saying to him. Surely, it was interesting. He'd never been bored in her company. She might not have had a formal education past her Philadelphia finishing school, a place she spoke of often, but she was well read and intelligent and would have done well in academics.

Just like his sister.

Rosalie strode arm in arm with Fletcher Lambert. He bent his head toward hers, and their soft laughter drifted through the icy air.

"Stop scowling." With a quiet laugh of her own, oddly accompanied by a wistfulness to her gaze, Charmaine elbowed his side. "They're in love. Do you think you should stand in their way with your grousing about it?"

"I wouldn't anyway."

"Don't be so sure about that. She's already turned him down once because she knows you disapprove."

Ayden stopped on the church steps to stare at her. "How do you know?"

"She told me."

"So my little sister confides in you." A little fist squeezed Ayden's heart. "She used to talk to me."

"She has me now that you've chosen to be unreasonable."

Rosalie looked so happy these days, perhaps he was being unreasonable.

"I'll think about changing my mind."

"You should." Charmaine glanced at her father. "Change your mind about interfering with others' hearts."

Focused on what Charmaine meant by that last remark, whether it was merely about Rosalie and Fletcher or someone else, Ayden didn't realize he ended up in the pew between Charmaine and Mia until changing places would have been awkward and too obvious.

Mia, however, didn't seem to notice him. She kept her attention either on the pastor or Gerrett Divine, sharing a hymnal and a Bible with him, keeping her shoulder turned in just enough to cut out Ayden.

He angled his shoulder away from her as well. That was how things should remain between them throughout the service. Afterward, she would go to his parents' house, and he would go to the Finney house.

Then Charmaine insisted Mia join them for dinner. "You must tell me all about Boston. I've been to every city on the coast except for Boston and so wish to go."

Don't accept, he urged her in silence.

But she agreed after only a moment's demur. "I'll be happy to tell you about Boston, and we can compare our impressions of New York and Philadelphia, too." Mia cocked her head, and her slanted eyes grew positively feline, an expression Ayden knew meant he should brace himself for the direct hit coming. "In return, I think you would be a fine foil to my article about women who choose to go to college alongside men, since you chose not to get an education and all."

"It wasn't really my choice." Charmaine bowed her head and peeked out through her extraordinary lashes. "My mother died, and Father needed a hostess."

"So you would go to college if you could?" Mia pressed.

Ayden grasped her elbow and nudged her toward the end of the pew. "At least refrain from pursuing your career on a Sunday." He leaned toward her and murmured, "And use your razor tongue on someone who can *reposte in tierce.*"

"*Seconde.*"

"You're slipping, Mia. You're better off reposting in tierce and par-rying in seconde."

"I prefer to parry in—"

"Don't tell me you fence, too, Miss Roper." Charmaine sounded so bored she nearly yawned.

Mia gave her a big-eyed look. "You don't fence?"

Charmaine shuddered. "Those blades of Ayden's rather terrify me."

"Have you managed to recruit any other females to learning the art?" Mia asked.

"One or two. Perhaps you should come interview them."

"I'd like that." Her face lit, all signs of strain and fatigue vanishing with one flash of her warm smile. "And perhaps I can persuade Miss Finney not to be afraid of the fencing blades. They're not dangerous when handled properly. Not any more dangerous than a butcher's knife and less so than an ax."

"You are so right." Charmaine looked more interested in his collection of weapons than she had any time he mentioned it.

Leave it to one female to communicate with another.

He started to thank her, but she headed away from him down the aisle. "I must speak to Genevieve. I'm interviewing her and some others tomorrow morning." She paused. "Then I'd like to find a way to get safely back to the train."

Ayden stepped into the aisle in front of her. "Not by yourself."

"Perhaps Deputy Lambert will take me when he's off duty. If Rosalie comes along—"

"I'll take you." Ayden smiled at Charmaine to assure her he wasn't abandoning her, then returned his attention to Mia. "I have classes in the morning, but after lunch, I will take you back to the train, if the sheriff says it's safe. Now hurry with Mrs. Baker. We must not keep Dr. Finney waiting on his dinner."

Ayden might as well not have been there for all the attention anyone paid him over the dinner table or coffee afterward. Dr. Finney asked

Mia innumerable questions about what she wrote. Charmaine and Mia talked about publications for ladies, about Boston culture, about an education versus staying at home.

"I believe the Lord calls each of us differently," Charmaine concluded. "We each have to examine our hearts and pray and see where the Lord leads us to go, whether in a career or marriage or taking care of a relative."

Ayden poised himself to kick Mia under the table if she started to argue. The preparation was unnecessary. A thoughtful look settled over her features, and she nodded.

"You make a good point." And from beneath the table, she drew out her portfolio and began to write.

"Euphemia Roper," Ayden snapped, "have you no manners?"

"Not when I need to remember something." She spoke around a pencil between her teeth.

Charmaine and her father emitted genuine laughs, not merely polite huffs of amusement to appease a slightly eccentric guest.

Later, while Mia assisted Charmaine in the kitchen, cleaning up as best she could with one hand, Dr. Finney cast Ayden a warm smile. "I confess I was wrong about her. She was a brilliant student, but I thought her a little vulgar for being so independent and traveling the eastern cities on her own. But she is quite charming as well as brilliant. If we had female professors at the college, she would be a fine asset to the staff."

"She'd think of something she wanted to remember and stop in the middle of a lecture to write it down on paper." Ayden meant to sound disparaging. Instead, he spoke with all the warmth and affection he wished he didn't feel for her.

Finney's eyes narrowed. "Perhaps we should have her stay here. Your house must be bursting at the seams."

"She might like that."

And so would he.

"I'll speak to my daughter about it," Finney said. "Now, since you chose to get shot at by counterfeit railroad guards yesterday instead of coming here, would you like to see that papyrus now?"

Ayden followed the older man into his office, which reeked of pipe smoke, and lost himself in ancient history for an hour. When he emerged, leaving Finney with his scroll, the early twilight was falling, and Charmaine suggested they leave before dark.

"The sky is so clear it's going to get terribly cold for walking." Charmaine laid her hand on Ayden's arm. "Will I see you tomorrow?"

"I don't think so." He plucked at the fold of his neck cloth to stop himself from giving in to the urge to push her hand off his arm. "I tutor on Monday nights. But perhaps Tuesday? I'd like to arrange a sledding party Tuesday or Wednesday. The children need exercise, and their parents need a respite. Will you help with that?"

"You know I will. Wednesday will be best."

The sledding party settled, Ayden offered Mia his arm and started for home. Neither of them spoke for the four-block walk between the Finney house and Ayden's. Mia clutched her portfolio as though it held all her worldly wealth, which perhaps it did, and Ayden no longer knew what to say to her. After her display in church, he expected her to continue honing her knives on Charmaine. Instead, the two of them parted on cordial, even warm, terms. Weren't they supposed to despise one another?

How self-centered of him. Of course, they had to be rivals for him. Apparently Mia had decided they were not. She truly no longer cared whom he wed. For some reason, that notion set his molars grinding and his heart feeling like a piece of cloth must beneath the blades of a pair of shears.

At the back door of the house, Mia turned to him and spoke at last. "I wish I didn't like her. If she were less kind and gracious or if she didn't have a warm heart, I could believe you only wished to marry her to advance your career. But she is all of those things, and I think perhaps you do love her more than you think."

He wanted to believe her. He wanted to believe he loved Charmaine Finney because she was kind and intelligent and beautiful. He enjoyed her company. She brought him peace and had soothed his still-bruised heart after Mia left. But the pressure her father placed on him always lay between them.

To Dr. Finney, Ayden was the son he never had, a man-child he could bring up to follow in his academic footsteps, a male in the family to whom he could leave the fortune he had inherited and built. Finney would interview other candidates for the professorship, but no one at the college would consider hiring an outsider when their own director's future son-in-law was there and qualified and beloved by his students.

For months, Ayden had tried to convince himself he was courting Charmaine because she was worth courting and nothing more. Then Mia appeared in the doorway of that train car, and the doubts began. And in the middle of those doubts, Dr. Finney pressured Ayden to make a commitment to Charmaine. He'd made it, too. He'd promised to offer for her. From what Mia had told him outside his family home, she had accepted his decision and gave it her blessing.

"But does it have yours, Lord?" He stood before the kitchen stove with its banked fire still allowing some warmth to radiate into the room. "I'm still not certain my staying here had your blessing, and I can't make that mistake again. I can't hurt another person like I did Mia."

No answer came to him. No peace washed over him. Fatigue weighed him down like a barrel of snow. With classes in the morning, he climbed the steps to the attic, where he slept until Ma's soft knock on his door woke him in time to see to the horses, dress in his formal teaching clothes, and head to campus.

After his first class, two female students approached him with tentative smiles and downcast eyes. "Professor Goswell," one of them spoke in a soft, breathy voice, "Dorothea and I would like to be interviewed by Miss Roper. Will you arrange it?"

"We promise to say only nice things about you." Dorothea Simon's voice never failed to startle Ayden, for it was almost mannishly deep in comparison to her petite, blonde femininity.

He grinned at them both, not in the least fooled by their demure behavior. "You may say what you like of me to Miss Roper. I'm sure she'll be happy to talk to you two and others. Thursday morning in the museum, if that's all right with her?"

He stowed his lecture notes in his office, then returned home to fetch the sleigh. Rosalie and the Herring children ran around the front lawn, rolling snow into enormous balls to form a snowman. Their cheeks glowed and their eyes sparkled, Rosalie's most of all.

She ran to him across the fluffy terrain and grabbed his hands. "Help us get this ball atop the others, or he'll be without a head."

"We're going to give him a carrot nothe." Roy gave Ayden a gap-toothed grin.

"Hey, when'd you lose that tooth?" Ayden gave the boy a playful punch on the shoulder.

"Thith morning."

"He talks funny now," Ellie said.

"Not for long." Ayden crouched to examine the head-sized lump of snow. "Let's see. I think I can lift this, but I'd like some help."

More hindrance than help, the two children got their mittened hands beneath the ball of snow, and Ayden hefted it atop the stout statue. The children and Rosalie danced around with glee. Smiling, Ayden continued toward the house.

"Thank you, Ayden." Rosalie waved to him, then dashed after him. "I almost forgot. Fletcher said there are deputies out at the train, so if you want to go looking, it's all right. He said they haven't found anything, but you're welcome to look in the cars that are still upright."

"Thank you. And thank Fletcher."

"Thank him yourself"—Rosalie's eyes flashed—"by being nice to him so he'll ask me to marry him."

"If that's what you want. If you're sure."

"I'm sure."

Studying the dreamy softness that came over her, Ayden believed her. She looked like he wished he felt about Charmaine. "All right. I'll be nice to him." He kissed her chilly cheek, then entered the house.

Ma and Mrs. Herring sat at the kitchen table, sorting through children's clothing and drinking coffee. The nameless little boy sat under the table, stacking and knocking down a pile of blocks Ayden recognized from his childhood.

He greeted the ladies, then asked, "Where's Mia?"

"She's in my sitting room, writing." Ma rose. "You look cold. Have some coffee and take her some. She's been in there for hours."

"Of course she has." He accepted the coffee for himself and for Mia, then crossed the hall to the sitting room, which was tucked between the dining room and the back of the house. It overflowed with flowered cushions, baskets of sewing, and more baskets of knitting, books, and piles of ladies' journals. At one end, Mia sat at a secretary, her bandaged left wrist cradled against her front, her right hand flying across a sheet of paper. She made no movement to indicate she noticed his entrance until he set the coffee directly in front of her.

"Thank you," she said, then continued to write.

"Would you like to go to the wreck?" he asked.

"Mmm." She set her pen down long enough to sip some coffee, then resumed her work.

"Fletcher says it's safe there."

"Mm."

Scratch, scratch, scratch went her pen.

"He doesn't think we should get shot at more than once or twice."

"Mm—what?" She dropped her pen and twisted around to face him. "What did you just say?"

Ayden grinned. "Trying to get your attention. We should leave for the wreck now so we don't lose the daylight."

"What time is it?" She glanced at a little enameled clock on the mantel, biting her lip and smoothing her right hand over her dark-green wool skirt. "Goodness, time has flown. Your mother must think me shockingly rude."

"My mother knows you better than that." He touched her shoulder. He shouldn't touch her, but she looked so unsure of herself, he wanted to give her some kind of comfort. "She knows you need to work. If you want to continue, I can go alone."

"No, I want to go if we won't get shot at again."

"Not with deputies there to guard it. They should have been there all along, but with all these people in town, they've been busy keeping things calm here, and they thought the train was safe."

"Those men were looking for something, and we were intruding." She looked down, plucking invisible lint or threads or something off her pretty dress. "They've probably already found it."

"Maybe not. We might have scared them off, too. I'll go hitch the horses." He drained his cup of coffee as he strode back through the kitchen. "We're off."

"Be careful." Ma met his gaze and held it long enough that he suspected she meant for him to be careful with more than the journey out to the wreck.

Be careful with Mia's heart? Be careful with his own?

Mia seemed bent on pretending she hadn't said anything about Charmaine the night before. She chattered in that sparkly, lively way he remembered too well, telling him about her morning's work.

"I interviewed Genevieve and a few others earlier this morning, then I started to write about the women students and what I've gleaned so far, but then words about the wreck kept intruding, so I've been writing about that instead. I think the editor will love a story about how the town has come together to help everyone stranded. You know, it's truly amazing. I'd forgotten how much people here care about one another."

"Unlike in the city?"

"I wouldn't say they don't care in the city. They just don't open their doors so trustingly. There are more people, so knowing whom to trust is more difficult. But here . . . you know which are the rotten apples right away." She stared at the portfolio she clutched on her lap, smoothing her fingers back and forth on the battered leather cover. "I didn't realize I missed it until I found myself back here, needing help."

Ayden stared at those smoothing fingers, something swelling inside his chest. "No one was particularly good to you the first four years you were here."

"People can't be good to you if you don't let them. The stationer offered to let me have all the pencils I wanted after that incident with Deputy Lambert catching me. But I wouldn't take charity. I burned sticks in the fire and wrote with the charcoal ends instead."

"Ah, Mia." Ayden leaned his head against the back of the sleigh seat. "Is that why you're so eager to get everything you have on your own? You're still that ridiculously proud sixteen-year-old girl with more pride than sense?"

And no family left, as the aunt had died five years ago, and the others had sent her away long ago.

"I think," she said by way of not responding to him, "that's the car I was in."

Ayden reined in and leaped out first this time, dropped the reins over a tree stump, and offered Mia a hand out of the sleigh. She set her portfolio on the seat, then clambered to the ground. Together, they strode through the drifts and hollows of snow to the abandoned car.

Ayden crouched at the edge of the car. "Let me lift you in."

He did and wished she were less scrawny beneath her heavy clothes, because he didn't want to worry about her taking good enough care of herself.

She hesitated in the doorway, then shook herself and led the way back through the car. "I was sitting here—ah, fifty cents." She snatched up the quarters and dropped them into her pocket.

"And a comb." Ayden fished it from beneath the seat.

They spent several minutes peering under and between the seats in search of dropped objects. They would take them to the church for passengers to collect. The rack above the seats appeared to be picked clean of luggage. Perhaps the passengers had taken it with them, good persons had collected it and taken it into town to be claimed, or thieves had been at work—likely a combination of all three.

"The wounded lady was back here." Mia moved to the space in front of the car's rear door. "I think she was coming after the child when the trains collided, and when she fell, she broke her leg."

"Then how'd she get away?"

"Someone took her out the back?"

Their eyes met.

"Why?" Ayden asked.

"And without the boy." Mia grasped the upper rack with her good hand and started to step onto a seat.

Ayden grasped her waist. "What are you doing?"

She froze. "Looking more thoroughly into the rack."

"I'll do it, but I'm tall enough to see there's nothing there."

"Not so much as a postage stamp?"

"Nothing."

Mia drew away from him and dropped to the floor, which was coated in frozen mud. "One last look beneath . . . the . . . seat . . ." Her voice trailed off on a kind of squeak.

"Are you hurt?" Ayden reached for her.

She evaded him and rocked back on her heels, waving a grubby white envelope in the air. "Wedged between the seat and the wall but not fallen all the way through. Should we open it?"

Her eyes shone as though someone had lit gas lamps behind them.

Ayden took the envelope from her and turned it over. "It's not sealed." His fingers shook, and his insides vibrated. "It might be nothing more than a shopping list."

"But you don't think so." She laughed. "Your eyes are sparkling."

He felt like a child on his birthday as he pulled up the flap of the envelope and drew out a single half sheet of paper. His breath snagged in his throat, and the blood drained from his head.

"What is it, Ayden?" Mia's face paled.

Ayden handed her the paper. "It looks like a ransom note."

Chapter Nine

Mia braced her feet on the front board of the sleigh and grasped the seat with her good hand. Those precautions barely kept her from sliding onto the floor during their wild ride back to Hillsdale. When they found no deputies around the train, Ayden seemed to throw caution to the wind and urged the horses to fly along the runner ruts in the snow. Wind whipped into Mia's face, stinging her cheeks. If she looked anything like Ayden, her face was as red as a freshly ripened strawberry. Long before they reached town, the stinging turned to numbness, and water from her eyes froze on her cheeks.

Broad Street, in the middle of the afternoon, had grown too crowded for speed. Grumbling about people afraid to drive their sleighs or wagons faster than a crawl, Ayden reined in the team to match the pace of the traffic.

"Shall I take you home first?" Those were the first words he had spoken to her since they agreed they needed to get the note to the sheriff as quickly as possible.

She glared at him. "Of course not. I'm a witness."

"But after the last encounter with Fletcher, I thought—"

"I wouldn't want to encounter any more arresting officers?" Her smile was stiff, brittle, the corners of her eyes tight. "I wasn't a serious criminal, you know. I only took pencils and paper, nothing more costly."

He drew up the horses. "Until you stole my heart." He intended the remark to tease her, make her laugh.

She wrapped her arms around her portfolio as though it protected her heart from any invasion, and lifted her chin. "Like the pencils, I gave it back. If you no longer have it to give away, it's none of my doing. Perhaps you lost it somewhere between breaking your word to me and your ambition." She stepped from the sleigh and spun away, sending her skirts swirling around her like a cloud.

Ayden reached her in two strides and slipped his hand beneath her elbow. "I thought you believed I love Charmaine Finney."

"I do. You do—with your head. That is still in excellent working condition and looking more handsome than ever. The two of you will make a fine pair at college socials and the faculty dinners."

"Could we save this for the fencing floor?"

"Date and time?"

"Thursday morning on campus. I have two victims for your pen there."

"I'll be there. And right now, we need to be here." She headed for the sheriff's office.

Different people milled around the warmth of the stove, and a middle-aged deputy stood behind the desk. Otherwise, the office remained the same—stuffy and odorous. The deputy showed no recognition of Mia but practically bowed to Ayden.

"How may I help you, Professor?"

"We need to speak to the sheriff right away." Ayden stuffed his hands into his coat pockets, and the note crackled.

"He's busy, but I'll see if he'll give you a minute." The deputy pushed through a door behind him.

Mia arched one brow at Ayden.

"His son is in one of my classes."

"Ah. I wondered at the reverence."

"Don't be absurd." The corners of Ayden's mouth twitched.

Mia looked away, her fingers pressed to her own lips as though doing so could shove back the memory of kissing him for the first time. The corners of his mouth had twitched then over something silly she'd said. Then, without warning, he leaned forward and—

"Professor Goswell, how may I help you?" The aging sheriff stood in the doorway to the back office.

"We need to talk in private." Ayden glanced toward the watchful, listening people near the stove.

The sheriff nodded his understanding and led them into a back room with a stove and hot coffee and straight-backed chairs. Ayden introduced Mia, and the sheriff gave her a hard look. "I've heard of you, Miss Roper."

"Yes, sir. I went to the college with your son."

"Ah, yes, good of you to return to us, though not here, I expect."

"No, it's not good." Mia perched on the edge of the chair and told the chief about finding the little boy right before the wreck.

He nodded as she spoke. "Mr. Goswell told me about it the other morning. I've put the word out here in town, but no one's come forward to claim him."

"We're here," Ayden said, "because we think we've found out why they haven't." He handed the sheriff the ransom note.

The man studied the half sheet of cheap paper, the block letters formed with what seemed to be a bit of coal for they smudged at the merest touch. Nonetheless, the message was clear: *Fifty thousand dollars if you want to see Jamie again.*

"Hmm." The sheriff laid the note on his desk and steepled his hands beneath his stubbly chin. "So how did you come across this?"

They told their stories again. The chief listened, nodded, and at the end, shook his head.

"You have no reason to believe this was tied to that child you found. After all, the ransom note was in the same train car. What good would it do there?"

"I expect whoever took him intended to mail it along the route to divert any hunters off the track," Mia suggested. "And it may be the reason someone shot at us the other day. They could have been looking for it."

The sheriff gave her a condescending smile. "That sounds like the sort of far-fetched idea a writer would come up with."

Mia stiffened. "I write true stories, sir, not fiction."

"Sir," Ayden said, rather too quickly, "this does add up, you know. An abandoned child, a ransom note found in the same area, a woman who has disappeared."

"Yes, indeed it does add up." The sheriff rose, grinning. "It adds up to a lot of melodrama for which I do not have time."

"Perhaps you should make time," Mia said through her teeth.

The sheriff's head jerked back as though she had slapped him. "Maybe I can send out some telegrams to my colleagues in other cities. But if a child had been abducted early enough to be on that train, you'd think we would have heard something before Thursday night, now wouldn't we, Miss Roper?"

Shoulders slumping, she nodded.

"Nonetheless"—the sheriff smiled—"I'll keep this just the same." He tucked the note into his desk, shook their hands, and escorted them back to the frigid afternoon air.

"The audacity." Mia quivered with her effort not to scream in frustration. "How dare he belittle me that way. It's all nonsense because I'm a writer. I've never written an untruth in my life. I'm a serious journalist who thinks falsifying stories is unethical and—"

Ayden laid a gloved finger across her lips. "You're drawing a crowd. Let's get back to my house, and we can discuss it."

They climbed into the sleigh and drove the few blocks to the Goswell house. But once they arrived, discussing anything seemed impossible. First Ayden needed to see to the horses, and in the house, Rosalie sat in the middle of the front parlor, lining up toy soldiers for the toddler. Charmaine sat on a sofa with a child on either side of her as she read fairy tales to them, and Mrs. Goswell, along with half a dozen other middle-aged women, stirred pots on the stove, rolled out pastry dough, and filled the circles of crust with meat and potato filling, creating the pasties Mrs. Goswell learned to make from her Cornish grandmother.

"Pasties." Mia spoke the word with awe. "I haven't had a pasty like these since I left here."

"Then you shouldn't have left us." Mrs. Goswell all but pushed her into a chair and set a steaming meat pie in front of her. "We're making these for the stranded passengers, so you deserve one. Did you eat lunch?"

"Not yet."

"And you barely touched any breakfast. Ayden, sit." She spoke as he entered the back door.

He paused in the doorway. "I see Charmaine is here. I should talk to her."

"She's occupied with the children right now." Mrs. Goswell dusted flour off the second kitchen chair. "Sit and tell us what you've been about all day."

Between bites of the succulent pastry, they told Ayden's mother and the other ladies about their hunt for the baby's people. They did not tell them about the ransom note. By silent agreement, they kept that information to themselves. No sense in alarming people or letting gossip spread through town and warn the kidnappers, if they were still around.

Of course they must be. Getting anywhere since the wreck would be difficult with the snow and blocked train tracks unless they managed to hire a sleigh or heavy wagon.

Finished with his pasty and the report of their activities, Ayden excused himself and left the kitchen. A few moments later, his compelling voice rippled from the parlor. He would be talking to Charmaine, perhaps making plans to take her out in the sleigh with no leather portfolio or past pain between them, only a bright future before them.

The meat pie dried in Mia's mouth. She took a long draft of milk to wash it down and nearly choked on the lump blocking her esophagus.

"Are you all right?" Mrs. Goswell leaned over the table and spoke in an undertone. "Do you need to lie down?"

Mia shook her head. Lying down would merely give her time alone to think of Ayden with Charmaine Finney, holding her hand, kissing her, perhaps. It would only give her too much time alone to remember the myriad details of the day that reminded her why she had fallen in love with Ayden.

She pushed back her chair. "I should do something useful, like finish writing up my notes in a legible form, unless, of course, I can be of use here?"

"We're almost done." Mrs. Goswell studied Mia with her brows knitted. "You may wish to wait a while before going into the sitting room. I banked the fire after you left, and it's got to be pretty cold in there."

"I'll be all right." Better off than she would be in the same room with Ayden and Charmaine.

Mia started for the door.

"Oh, wait," Mrs. Goswell called. "I also forgot to tell you that the laundry came back today, and we found embroidery inside that little boy's clothes. Probably his initials."

Mia gripped the doorframe and turned back slowly. "What are they?" She posed the question in a strained whisper.

All the ladies stopped rolling and stirring to stare at her.

"It's JMY," Mrs. Goswell said. "Worked in fine stitching on every piece of his clothes."

"JMY," Mia repeated, her blood roaring through her ears. "Jamie."

With no consideration for good manners, she shoved through the kitchen door, allowing it to bang shut behind her, then raced down the hall to the parlor and flung open the door. "Jamie?"

Ayden looked up from the book he read to the children, his eyes a deep, sharp blue. Charmaine raised perfectly arched golden brows in query. The two older children's mouths dropped open. Giving a start, Rosalie knocked over the row of soldiers.

"Jamie." Mia dropped to her knees on the rug. "Will you come to Aunt Mia, Jamie?"

A grin spreading across his face, the abandoned little boy from the train toddled toward Mia.

Chapter Ten

*A*yden surged to his feet. "What did you just call him?"

"Jamie." Mia crouched and held her uninjured hand out to the little boy.

He wobbled toward her on chubby legs, reaching out to her with that grin. "Momma."

She gathered him against her. "Not yet, but we will find her soon, little one."

"How did you ever discover his name?" Charmaine looked dubious.

"His initials." Mia held Ayden's gaze, her eyes wide and intense. "JMY. It's sewn on all his clothes."

"But it could have been anything else." Rosalie stood. "Jack, Jacob, Joseph . . . I'm sure there are a lot more names. But you pick Jamie, and it's the right one."

"It seems," Charmaine murmured, "Miss Roper has special talents."

"Not particularly. With the *y* and all . . ." She still looked straight at Ayden, as though expecting him to say something.

Saying nothing seemed like the best course to him—nothing about the ransom note, in any event. The fewer people who knew of the abduction, the better.

"Momma," the baby said again.

"That's the first thing he's said," Ellie cried.

Roy's lower lip protruded. "I hope nothing terrible happened to her."

"I don't think it has," Ayden said. "It's likely that the woman with the broken leg was a neglectful nursemaid who's afraid to come forward now."

A nursemaid hired by the criminals?

"Are you all right taking care of him, Mia, Rosalie?" Ayden asked. "That is, neither of you has any experience with small children."

"We love Miss Rosie," Ellie said.

Roy gave Rosalie an adoring look. "She's tho pretty."

Everyone laughed, except Roy, who turned pink.

"I'm getting practice for when I have my own." Rosalie grinned at him.

He frowned at her. "Not for at least half a decade."

"When I'm too old?"

"Ahem." Mia grimaced. "That would make you twenty-four, which is two years younger than I am."

"And rather old to be marrying and setting up your nursery," Charmaine said.

Ayden twisted his head and stared at her. Even if she weren't a mere year younger than Mia, she wasn't usually inclined to such spiteful remarks. "Charmaine, shall I walk you home? I find I need to go out again."

"Please." Charmaine rose in one fluid motion. "You'll stay for dinner with us. Your house is so crowded."

"Always stealing my brother when I wanted him to—" Rosalie broke off on a sigh.

Ayden narrowed his eyes as he rose. "Dinner sounds like an excellent idea, if it's not interfering with something else."

"It's not." Rosalie's lips turned down. "Children, let's go see if my ma can spare some early supper for you two."

She gathered Ellie and Roy and left the parlor.

"And we should be going. It's nearly dark out." Ayden strode to the door. He needed to get away from Mia and the sight of her holding that little boy against her. If she'd married him, they would have had their own child by now, or at least—

He yanked his mind from such inappropriate thoughts and left the parlor to retrieve Charmaine's fur wraps. He intended to walk her home, then go to the sheriff again and let him know about the initials in the boy's clothes. That was something more the sheriff could telegraph to other lawmen, before Ayden partook of a hasty dinner with the Finneys, then moved on to tutor some of his students.

"Will you ask Rosalie to come to my house tomorrow?" Charmaine was saying when Ayden returned to the parlor. "She and I can finalize details for the sledding party, perhaps bake some cookies."

"I'd be happy to help if I didn't have appointments with a few of my classmates." Mia spoke from where she half lay on the floor, marching soldiers up and down, much to Jamie's delight.

If the trains had been running, Ayden would have taken both Mia and Jamie aboard and spirited them to someplace safer than his home, where his open and warm family welcomed everyone. He needed to warn her—warn them—without giving anything away to his family.

"Mia." He crouched so only she would hear.

"You're getting my coat on the floor," Charmaine protested.

"Mia," Ayden said, "be wary of strangers."

She sat up so fast her forehead nearly collided with his nose. "You're right. I hadn't thought of that, but—yes, no strangers."

"But what if his family comes to claim him?" Charmaine asked. "They'll be strangers."

"No one," Ayden reiterated.

Mia nodded, her mouth grim.

Charmaine's mouth was grim, too. She said nothing, not even "Good evening" to Mia as Ayden held her coat for her, and she secured her hat atop her crown of curls. She said nothing until they reached the path shoveled through the snow for pedestrians. Then she gripped Ayden's arm hard and turned her stern expression toward him. "What, may I ask, was that all about?"

"What all about?"

"Don't play coy with me, Mr. Goswell. It's unattractive, and you're too intelligent to play games."

He still looked at her blankly.

She sighed, forming a cloud of her breath before her face. "That little tête-à-tête on the floor with Miss Roper."

"It has to do with the child, but I can't share with you."

"I see." Charmaine bowed her head and tramped on in silence, save for the crunch of their footfalls on the crust of the snow. A block from her house, she glanced up again. "I haven't objected to you running around with Miss Roper. I know you are old friends, and she was practically a member of your family for many years. But, well, it does look rather bad for me. People talk in this town."

Ayden's stomach twisted. "Would you prefer I not see her any more than absolutely necessary?"

"Of course I'd rather you not see her any more than necessary or at all. She's everything you admire in a lady—beauty and intelligence and an education."

"But not loyalty. She chose a career over me."

"Ah." Charmaine's eyes widened. "So you would rather have a wife with no career ambitions of her own."

Ayden opened his mouth to say yes but shut it again. If he said Charmaine was right, then he would stop her from pursuing her own interests, which would surely make her life and thus *her* dull. If he said she was wrong, then he sounded as though he disapproved of her life as little more than a fine hostess for her father and organizer of one or more charitable events a year. If he didn't want a lady who chose to follow her interests, even if those interests meant working at something beyond being a wife, mother, and hostess for him, then he appeared absurd for courting and proposing marriage to Mia in the first place.

"I should warn you." Charmaine filled in the silence. "I am ambitious. When my father said I had to leave Philadelphia and become his hostess instead of . . . continuing on in the city, I decided then that I would become the first lady of the college before more than a decade or so passes."

"I'm afraid your father may be getting too old for that position."

"Not Father." She shot him a coy glance from beneath her lashes.

"You expect me to be president of the college?" Ayden's laugh sounded hollow. "Let me get hired as a permanent professor first."

"You know that is all but official already anyway."

After he proposed to her.

His stomach twisted again. "I'm not counting any chicks before I see the eggs." They reached the Finney house, and he paused on the stoop. "I have an errand to run, but I'll return for dinner."

"All right." Still somber, Charmaine entered the house and closed the door without looking at him again.

Feeling as though the piles of snow along walkways and drives had packed themselves into his boots, Ayden tramped to the sheriff's office. The same deputy at the counter didn't even ask his business; he immediately escorted Ayden into the back office.

"I just sent Lambert to fetch you," the sheriff greeted Ayden. "Did you meet him along the way?"

"No, but I expect he'll be happy to go to my house anyway. What's wrong?"

"This." The sheriff held up a sheet of flimsy telegraph paper. "It seems that a child has been abducted."

"What?" Ayden snatched the telegram from the sheriff.

The message had apparently arrived only minutes before the train wreck. Its message was concise and clear. A child named James Matthew Yardley of Pittsburgh had been taken from his home on Wednesday.

Authorities were spreading the word far and wide the longer the child went missing.

"We didn't get the word until a quarter hour ago," the sheriff explained. "Seems when the wreck happened, the telegrapher completely forgot about this." He grimaced. "As though anyone could forget about something like this. Then he had so many messages dealing with the wreck and passengers this one got lost."

Ayden opened the door to ensure no one was within listening range, then closed it and turned back to the sheriff. "He answers to the name Jamie."

He explained about the initials in the child's clothing and how he had responded to Mia calling him Jamie.

"Then you need to bring him to us," the sheriff declared.

"Here? The sheriff's office is going to take in a little boy. Where will you keep him? A jail cell?" Ayden couldn't keep the sarcasm from his tone.

The sheriff scowled. "I was thinking my house. He could be in danger."

"With your wife home alone when she's there?" Ayden shook his head. "Sir, he's much safer in our house. It's full of people right now."

"Mostly females."

"Would you want to tangle with my mother?"

The sheriff laughed. "She should know the danger. And don't you have other children there?"

"We do." Ayden sighed. "As well as your youngest deputy, more than I like."

"And he'll be there even more than you like if I agree to you keeping this boy." The sheriff tapped his fingers on his desk, then nodded. "Why don't you talk to your family and Miss Roper. If they agree, then you can move that other lady and her two children into our house so as not to cause any risk for them. When Lambert returns, I'll send him back with you."

"If it means Lambert will be around more often, I know what Rosalie will say." The corners of Ayden's mouth twitched.

He was getting the message loud and clear—stop trying to manage Rosalie's heart for her. If their parents approved, opposing her choice for a mate would only damage his relationship with his sister. His smile faded quickly, though. Needing to take these steps meant he would have to cancel dinner with the Finneys.

"Will you send Lambert to the Finney house? I have to go tell Charmaine I won't be staying for dinner after all." And he couldn't tell her why.

Unfortunately, her father had come home to hear the announcement. While Charmaine's face showed no expression, Dr. Finney's turned the color of a plum.

"I don't appreciate you disappointing my daughter, Ayden, especially if it has anything to do with the train riffraff."

"It has nothing to do with riffraff from the train or elsewhere." For good measure, in the event Finney did not receive the message strongly enough, Ayden added, "Nor does it have anything to do with Miss Roper."

"Hmm. Well"—Finney still scowled—"I suppose if this is a family matter, you are not able to share, but you must later. I do not like secrets between courting couples or Charmaine being left here alone for an evening. She is young. She should have a host of people around her."

"Then you should have left me in Philadelphia," Charmaine muttered.

Ayden gave her a sharp glance, one eyebrow raised.

"What was that?" Finney demanded.

"Nothing, Papa." Face flushed, Charmaine laid her hand on her father's arm. "I'm just urging you to drop the matter. If Ayden said he has something important to do this evening, he has something important to do this evening. I'll punish him by making him help bake cookies tomorrow for the sledding party on Wednesday."

"Sledding party?" Dr. Finney's brow puckered. "What sledding party?"

Ayden shot Charmaine a look of gratitude for changing the subject. "Something I thought we and some of the students could do for the children from the train. They're restless from being shut in for days."

"Hmph. I have no authority to stop the students or you from doing something so foolish," Finney said, "but you will not attend, Charmaine. It's too undignified for a lady about to be married."

"But, Papa, I dearly love sledding." Her face turned so pink and her lower lip quivered so much Ayden sought for something to make her smile.

He took her smooth white hand between both of his, which were still clad in gloves. "You and I will go on a private sledding party on Saturday. Would that suit?"

"I'd love that, Ayden." She smiled, all right. Her perfect teeth flashed, and her eyes lit to a startling blue.

Her father smiled, too. "Most suitable, especially by Saturday."

When they would be engaged.

The notion should please him, fill him with the excitement and anticipation he had felt before—and after—he proposed to Mia. Instead, a hard ball of anxiety wound through his gut. This felt more like when he told Mia he would not be going east with her.

A knock sounded on the door, and, for the first time since the deputy began to court Rosalie, Ayden was happy to see him.

Chapter Eleven

*B*y Tuesday afternoon, when Mia had heard nothing from the
sheriff regarding Jamie or even from Ayden, who had managed
to leave earlier than breakfast preparation, Mia decided to take action
on her own. It wouldn't be the first time she had investigated a probable
crime after lawmen seemed too slow or altogether disinclined to do so.

Bundled in her hooded coat, boots, and gloves, she told Mrs.
Goswell she was going out, then tramped through the frozen slush and
biting wind to the telegraph office. Inside, the depot steamed from a
kettle whistling atop the stove, and the telegraph machine chattered like
a collection of squirrels. At his desk, the telegrapher raised one finger
to signal he would be with her in a minute without stopping his con-
tinual motion with the key. Instinctively, Mia listened to the dots and
dashes coming down the wires. She had learned Morse code when writing about women telegraphers. The messages she managed to decipher
sounded like frantic communications to and from passengers stranded
there in Hillsdale. One or two sounded angry, a father's demand for
his daughter to come home, as though she could obey without a train
to carry her. Another was from a frantic wife, and a third to a husband

who seemed not to understand why his wife hadn't simply gotten on the next train.

She supposed she was as good as eavesdropping, but this was work, grist for her journalistic mill to grind down into a story. Nothing was wrong with seeking information. She didn't know names to reveal. Yet she turned away from the telegrapher to pretend she was not listening to the messages, as though she were ashamed.

And as her eyes scanned the room, she noticed a man in a railroad uniform tucked in a corner behind the stove, his hands wrapped around a cup. Apparently he had come into the depot to warm himself. Yet something about his appearance, the tilt of his head, the way he raised the cup, struck a note of familiarity.

She took a step back, considering leaving to return at another time, but the telegrapher called to her, and running would have looked more suspicious than staying.

"I have one telegram to send to a number of people." She pulled a sheet of paper from her portfolio and laid it on the desk. "How soon can you get these out?"

"We get them out immediately, miss." The telegrapher smiled at her. "But this will cost you."

"Of course."

And worth every penny if she got good answers—or any answers. She would make the money back and then some once she sold the article.

She paid the fee. With a surreptitious glance back, she left the depot to return to the Goswell house and her writing. The slush seemed more difficult to navigate on the walk home, the air colder. She tucked her chin into her collar and trudged on. In Boston, she would have been able to stay that way no matter how long her walk. In Hillsdale, half a dozen people called to her. Most simply greeted her. Two wanted to chat. An acquaintance from college expressed delight in seeing her return to Hillsdale, then rushed off to her job inside the stone courthouse collecting documents from attorneys and making certain they reached the right persons for cases to be filed or settled.

As Mia continued toward the church, someone else called to her. She paused and saw the stationer approaching her, a knitted cap low enough on his forehead it nearly covered his gray eyebrows. Mia's stomach performed a few pirouettes.

"I haven't been near your shop, Mr. Phelps. Promise." She grinned at him.

He laughed loudly enough for the bark to echo off the buildings. "You know you're welcome any time now. But I saw you and thought I'd bring you these to help write those stories I've been hearing about." He fished in the capacious pocket of his overcoat and withdrew a handful of pencils.

Mia's laugh was the one to ring around the street this time. Passersby stopped to smile or stare, including a man a hundred feet away, whom she swore looked like the railroad worker from the telegraph office, but when she turned her head to get a better look, the man had vanished between two buildings.

She returned her attention to the stationer. "You are so gracious."

"Well, my dear child, if we don't forgive people who do wrong, we will lose our humanity."

"Thank you." She kissed him on the cheek, tucked the pencils inside her portfolio, and bade him good-bye.

Forgiveness. That was the problem—she could not forgive Ayden for betraying her heart. *If only he would ask for forgiveness instead of acting as though he didn't need it.*

But all those years ago, Mr. Phelps hadn't said anything about the person asking for mercy. He had urged the lawman to let her go while she was still defiant about her minor theft. That was something to ponder . . . but not now. For now, she wanted to look out for that railroad worker who appeared so familiar.

All the way home, Mia kept glancing over her shoulder. Although she saw no one, she decided to tell Ayden or Fletcher.

Neither Ayden nor Fletcher arrived at the Goswell house before Mia climbed to her room. Neither did she see them the next morning. She thought about paying a call on the sheriff, but considering how he'd dismissed her notions earlier, she suspected he would simply lay her suspicions down to too much imagination.

She holed up in the sitting room instead of worrying about vanishing railroad workers and began to write her articles. By midafternoon, her article on the train wreck and the aftermath of how the town came together to help the stranded passengers was finished. As for her articles on women students, she would finish that the next day, after her meeting with the two students who requested her to interview them. While she awaited information on the abducted child, she began to write the article. By Friday, when she got onto an eastbound train, she could send a telegram to her editor and inform the lady she was returning with three articles in hand.

By Friday, the sheriff could return the child to his family. By Friday, Ayden and Charmaine would be engaged. By Friday, Rosalie and Fletcher would be engaged. By Friday, all would be well.

All would be well with everyone except Mia. Her work in Hillsdale would be done, and she would return to Boston, her heart breaking all over again.

Maybe if she made friends, life would not be so lonely during the few hours she wasn't working. People at church were friendly enough, but being a single female making her own way in the world was difficult when most ladies lived at home or with husbands.

Being a single female was difficult in Hillsdale. Her college classmates who lived there had all married. Some still worked outside their homes. Others, like Genevieve, had found ways to use their education in their homes. All seemed content with their places in life.

"I thought I was, too." Mia rubbed her right wrist with her left hand. "I'm getting everything I want."

So why did she feel like laying her head on the desk and weeping or running through the snow until she no longer possessed the strength to weep?

The answer lay before her in the neatly written pages of her article on the wreck. For eighteen months, she had kept herself too busy to remember the warmth of being part of a family, a community. In less than a week, the warmth of the Goswell family, the generosity of the townspeople, and the realization that she need only be alone because she chose to be had drawn her back to safety like a momma cat shooing her wandering offspring home. For the first time in a year and a half, Mia felt sheltered and loved as she hadn't felt since Ayden told her he wasn't going to Boston after all.

Ayden didn't love her enough. He loved his career more.

Mia glanced at the neatly stacked papers on the secretary and smiled with a twist to her lips. "Nor did you love him enough or you would have stayed."

For eighteen months, she had blamed Ayden for not going with her. He had blamed her. They had both been wrong, and now the damage was done. Ayden would be engaged in a few days, and she would no longer have to chase story after story to make a respectable living for herself. She would receive a salary. She might even be able to purchase a little house.

A week ago, that idea sounded wonderful. She could have a cat or two, grow flowers, prepare her own meals when she liked—after coming home to a building void of other human voices with which to converse, someone with whom she could share the joys or sorrows of her day.

A knock sounded on the sitting room door, and Rosalie called, "Coming out to sled with us?"

A cottage void of someone asking her to come out and play. She hadn't played since her last summer in Michigan, when the Goswell family had taken her along to Lake Michigan to sail and fish in the crystal-clear blue water and bask in sunshine on the sugary sand.

"Yes, I'm coming." Mia set a book on the completed article to keep it from being knocked on the floor and scattered or damaged and opened the door to a sparkling-eyed Rosalie.

Rosalie seized her arms and hugged her. "I'm so glad you're coming. Remember the last time we went sledding?"

"Didn't we end up breaking the sled and nearly our necks on a tree?"

"And Pa forbade me to ever go sledding without Ayden again." Rosalie executed a pirouette in the middle of the hall, nearly knocking down a wall sconce with her outstretched arms. "I wonder if he'll change his mind about that once I'm married." She sang the last word, then scampered to the steps. "Come up to our room. I've found an old skirt you can wear so you don't get your good clothes dirty or risk damaging them."

"Rosalie, you're at least three inches taller than I am." Protesting, Mia followed nonetheless.

"I haven't always been. This is old, but it's a delicious deep pink, so it will look lovely on you. Ma had it packed in lavender in the attic. I don't think she gets rid of anything."

"And a good thing that was with little Jamie here." Mia hesitated on the landing. "Will he be all right here?"

"Fletcher says we need to carry on as though nothing out of the ordinary is happening." Rosalie laughed at Mia's start. "Of course he told me. We don't have secrets." She lifted her skirt and charged up the second flight, calling back, "I learned from Ayden that keeping secrets from one's intended is a terrible idea."

The crux of the gulf between Mia and Ayden. He hadn't confided in her that he didn't want to leave Hillsdale or why. That he hadn't wanted to leave didn't matter as much as why he hadn't told her. Now she would never know.

Ayden, with Charmaine's assistance, had avoided interacting with her for two days. When he hadn't been teaching classes or tutoring students at risk of failing his courses, he had been at Charmaine's house, even assisting in baking pastries to serve hungry college students and children during the sledding party.

"You are so right." Mia spoke too softly for Rosalie to hear her.

She joined Ayden's sister in the room they were sharing. Rosalie had laid out a dress with the wide, ruffled skirt from a few years earlier. Although it was heavy cotton instead of wool, the layers of petticoats and ruffles would make it warm.

"Hurry." Rosalie danced from foot to foot as though she were ten and not nearly twenty. "Fletcher will be here to escort us in just a few minutes."

Mia began to hurry out of her pretty but practical blue wool dress with its buttons up the front. "He's going sledding with us?"

"Probably not actually sledding. He'll be there to see that nothing rough occurs. The college boys can get a bit rowdy at times. Here, let me help." Rosalie sent the folds of the pink dress billowing over Mia's head. "I'll do up the buttons for you. You are so pretty, Mia. Did I tell you Charmaine isn't coming?"

Mia stiffened her face to keep her expression neutral. "Why not?"

"Her father doesn't approve." Rosalie took on an affected tone. "She may go sledding alone with Ayden after he proposes to her. Otherwise, this is too undignified."

"I see." Mia's fingers fumbled with buttons on the dress sleeves. "Then I presume Ayden isn't either?"

"I hope so. He has the sled. Now hurry, hurry, hurry."

By the time Fletcher Lambert rang the front bell, Mia and Rosalie were swathing themselves in hats and scarves and mittens.

The deputy glanced from one of them to the other and laughed. "I can't tell the two of you apart."

"I'm taller." Rosalie kissed his cheek.

He turned red and pretended to fend her off. "Bold wench."

She laughed. He laughed. They looked so happy Mia's insides cracked like limestone beneath a hammer's blow. The suggestion that perhaps she should stay home hovered on her lips. As though she read that thought, Rosalie grasped Mia's hand and dragged her outside.

It was a cold, clear afternoon with an inch or two of new snow from the night before turning everything a sparkling white. The snowman Rosalie had built with the Herring children had lost his hat to a burden of snow. Mia paused to pick up the battered felt hat and placed it atop the sculpture's pate. When she straightened, she caught sight of Rosalie and Fletcher stealing a quick kiss beside a massive maple tree in the front yard, and from the corner of her eye, she noticed a shadow flickering around the end of the house.

"Deputy?" she called to Lambert softly.

He jumped away from Rosalie as though she'd shouted. "Yes, ma'am?"

"It might be a trick of the light, but I believe I just saw someone sneaking around the side of the house."

Mia barely got the words out before Lambert sprinted across the snowdrifts to the front corner of the house. He stopped to examine the ground, then took off running.

Rosalie rolled her eyes and shrugged. "I had best get used to this sort of thing." She looked at Mia, concerned. "Do you think it's someone dangerous?"

"I don't know, but perhaps we should stay here." She turned toward the house.

Fletcher Lambert appeared around the house again, mopping his brow with his sleeve and scowling. "He had snowshoes. I couldn't keep up."

"Just a youth playing a trick, perhaps?" Mia asked.

"I expect so, but why don't you ladies go on to the sledding alone? I'll stay here for a while and join you later."

Mia glanced at Rosalie, expecting to see disappointment or even annoyance. Instead, the younger lady was gazing at her intended with adoration. "You be careful, Fletch." She blew him a kiss, then linked arms with Mia. "Let's be on our way before everyone else is having fun except for us."

"If you're sure." Mia glanced back at the deputy tramping around the perimeter of the house. He waved her off.

"He takes his work seriously." Rosalie poked Mia in the ribs. "As you found out."

"He told you about my misspent youth?"

"He did, but I never told Ayden."

"He knows now and likely considers himself lucky to have gotten out of marrying me."

"Not lucky if he marries Charmaine. Did you notice those claws she displayed the other day?"

They laughed and chatted as they made their way through the snow, sliding and holding one another up.

Two are better than one because they have a good reward for their labor. For if they fall, the one will lift up his fellow: but woe to him that is alone when he falleth, for he hath not another to help him up.

The verses from the fourth chapter of Ecclesiastes ran through Mia's head. In Boston, she had acquaintances, but no one who would hold her up if she fell. If her work dried up, no one would be there to give her food and shelter until she found other employment. If she fell ill or injured herself, no one would be there to care for her needs.

There in Hillsdale, people cared. She had neglected them for a year and a half out of hurt and anger at the town that kept her beloved in its clutches, yet they welcomed her with all the warmth and love of the father of the prodigal son.

All except for Ayden. He had opened his arms to another woman.

Mia's laughter died, and if Fletcher Lambert had been there with Rosalie, Mia might have gone back to the house. But he wasn't, and the shrieks and laughter from the sledding site reached them long before they rounded a curve in the road and found the familiar snow-clad hill descending before them.

And Ayden stood near them, with the Herring children tucked up on the sled, ready for a nudge down the gentlest part of the slope. "Hang on tight, kids."

He pushed. The runners bit, caught, and carried the sled sailing down the hill to the accompaniment of shrieks of glee. Ayden ran after them to help them make the climb up with the heavy wooden sled.

Halfway up the incline, he caught Mia's gaze upon him. His eyes widened, looking extraordinarily blue against the backdrop of white snow and distant pinewoods. For a moment, he didn't move. For a moment, Mia didn't breathe. Beside her, Rosalie giggled, then ran forward to pick up little Ellie, who was struggling to manage the last yards of the hill. And then Ayden reached the top, repositioning the sled for another run, his back to Mia.

She expelled her breath in a sigh intended to lift the weight upon her heart. Through the vapor swirling before her face, she watched Rosalie put the children on the sled, then squeeze herself on behind them.

"No need to follow us," she called to her brother. "I've got them."

They sped off down the hill, and Ayden stood a mere yard from Mia with two score or more of college students and children racing, slipping, and dodging around them.

"You'll want the steeper side of the hill," Ayden said.

"I'll wait for Rosalie, then." Mia backed up a step.

"She'll stay here with the children. Where's Lambert?"

"Someone went running around the corner of the house right before we left. He thought he should wait and keep an eye on things."

Ayden took a step toward her, closing the distance between them so no one could overhear. "Someone after Jamie?"

Mia crossed her arms over her middle. "Possibly. Enough of a possibility he thought he should stay."

"Should I go back, too?"

Mia narrowed her eyes and pressed her lips together.

Ayden grinned. "I know that look. What did I say to annoy you?"

Mia shrugged and started to turn away. A hundred feet from her, the young woman introduced to her on Sunday as Liberty Judd of Chicago stood dispensing hot beverages near a roaring fire. Mia could make a great deal of hay in shining sunlight if she spent time with the college girl and the others who approached her for refreshments. But as she took her first step toward the younger women, she decided she was not yet done with what she had to say to Ayden and swung back, her hands on her hips. "You haven't taken any interest in the child's safety for two days because you've been so occupied with advancing your career. Oh, wait, I meant to say courting your lady. So why are you running back there now? Because sledding with riffraff like me and your own sister, not to mention a Judd and Divine of Chicago, aren't good enough for her?"

Ayden's head jerked back as though she'd struck him on the chin. "That was uncalled for, Euphemia Roper. Yes, Charmaine isn't here because her father thinks it's too unruly a crowd for her sensibilities, but I'm here. I happen to enjoy a rowdy crowd."

Cheeks heating, Mia ducked her head. "That will make for a difficult future with Charmaine."

"Her father forbade it, and she still lives under his roof."

Mia cocked her head to one side and gave him an oblique glance. "You think she'd be here otherwise?"

"Of course." Ayden didn't meet her gaze. "We have our own sledding outing scheduled for Saturday."

"Sans riffraff." Mia sighed and stomped her feet. "I'm either going to join Miss Judd at the fire or go sledding. Standing around is making me cold."

She had said all she wanted and likely a lot more than she should have.

"Will there be a sled I can use over at the steeper hill?" she asked.

Ayden laughed. "Mia, a lady who looks like you do will have no trouble finding college boys willing to push you down the hill. But if you wait, I'll use ours. The children need to go warm up. They've been here for a while."

"There's no need. I'm sure I'll enjoy myself with the college boys." She started for the other side of the hill, where the land sloped at a more precipitous angle.

The instant she reached the summit, a half dozen youths surrounded her.

"We have our sixth lady," one of them cried. "Miss Roper, will you form a team with me?"

"Are we racing?" A frisson of excitement ran through Mia. "I haven't raced on a sled in years." Her last winter in Hillsdale, she was tucked up on the sled with Ayden. "I was a champion here, you know."

She allowed the shouting youths and giggling girls to hustle her forward to the line of sleds, poised for flight.

"Mia, wait," Ayden yelled above the tumult.

She clambered onto the end sled. A laughing youth slung himself on behind her.

"Henry Powers," Ayden bellowed, "don't—"

"Ready, set, go!" The cry for start drowned Ayden's shout.

Someone shoved them off the lip of the hill. Beaten down from hundreds of runners before them, the track was slick as ice. No friction slowed the runners. Wind whipped into Mia's face. She closed her eyes against the sting and gave herself up to the flight, the speed, the exhilaration of rocketing forward. Her companion emitted a sound like a war whoop. Mia laughed aloud, mouth open wide, for the first time since she couldn't remember. This had to go into her article somehow, these moments of sheer exuberance—

The left runner struck something solid and immovable. The sled spun sideways, backward, sideways again. Sky, sledders, and trees far too close twirled by once, twice. Mia's breath snagged in her throat. Her companion and she leaned one way and then the other, trying to stop the momentum.

The back right quarter of the sled slammed into the trunk of a spruce tree. The equipage flipped over, disgorging its passengers.

Mia sprawled on the snow, too winded to move.

"Miss Roper." Her companion leaned over her, patting her cheek. "Miss Roper? Are you all right?"

"If she is, it won't be because of you." Ayden shouldered the youth aside. "What were you thinking, sledding that close to the tree line? Mia?" He knelt beside her. "Mia, can you hear me?"

She tried to drag in a breath to tell him she could hear him fine, along with a few screams and too many tramping feet.

"Mia." Ayden sat cross-legged on the snow and propped her head on his knee. "Can you open your eyes?"

She managed a gasping "Yes," but kept her eyes shut. She didn't want to observe the score of people she was sure stared at her.

"Let her have some air." Ayden lifted her to a sitting position in the crook of his arm. "You especially, Henry. Be glad you're not in one of my classes this quarter."

"Sir, I—"

Mia waved her arm. "Don't . . . mad . . . him." Her breath came marginally easier. "I should . . . noticed." She dragged in a painful breath, but oxygen nonetheless. "Truly." She opened her eyes to find the crowd tramping up the hill with the sleds and Ayden's face close enough for the warm fog of his breath to brush against her lips.

"Thank goodness you're all right, Mia. When I saw you lying there . . ." His face grew closer.

She closed her eyes. Her lips parted, and her breath ceased again, this time due to her racing heart, the anticipation, the longing. With one more beat of her galloping pulse—

"Ayden! Ayden!" Rosalie ran down the hill, slipped, and slid the rest of the way on her seat. "Ayden, we've got to go home. Someone tried to take Baby Jamie."

Chapter Twelve

*A*yden sprinted for the house, Rosalie and Mia somewhere behind him. He needed the run, the distraction, the worry over Ma and the kidnapped baby to take his mind off of how he had come a hair's breadth from kissing Mia.

What was he thinking?

He hadn't been thinking. For a moment, while they sat on the snow and he cradled her in his arm, time had slipped backward, and she was the woman he had intended to marry, a lady he had the right to kiss on a snowy hillside.

Reaching his house, he slammed his fist onto the door handle and his shoulder into the heavy panel. It didn't budge. Of course not. It would be locked up tight.

"Ma, it's me, Ayden." He pounded his fist on the door harder than necessary. "Ma, open—"

The door swung inward, and Ayden tumbled across the threshold, nearly knocking down his father. "Sorry, Pa. Is Ma all right? Is the baby all right?"

"We're all fine now." Pa rested a steadying hand on Ayden's shoulder. "They're in the kitchen with the sheriff."

Ayden headed for the kitchen. Behind him, Rosalie, Mia, and Fletcher Lambert crowded into the front hall, chattering and asking questions.

Ma sat at the kitchen table with a cup of tea in front of her. Coffee sat before the sheriff, and Jamie appeared to be sleeping in a pallet of blankets as close to the stove as was safe.

Ayden stopped behind Ma's chair and grasped her shoulders. "You're all right. What happened?"

"Not as much as could have." The sheriff rose at the entrance of the other ladies. "Miss Roper saw someone lurking about, and because of that and Deputy Lambert staying, we were ready for trouble."

"Jamie was asleep upstairs, like the lamb he is," Ma said, "when somebody knocked on the door. I opened it, and there was a man in a railway uniform."

"Why did Lambert let her open the door?" Ayden glared at his future brother-in-law.

Fletcher frowned at him. "I thought it best to look like nothing was afoot."

"So wise of you." Rosalie looked at him with cow eyes.

Ayden managed not to gag, but when he met Mia's gaze by accident, he couldn't suppress a snort of mirth.

"It was the right thing to do," the sheriff said.

"What did he say he wanted?" Ayden asked.

"He said he had orders to take charge of the child who'd lost his family." Ma wrinkled her long, thin nose. "As though I would fall for such a tale. So I told him I had no idea what he was talking about and tried to slam the door in his face."

"He slammed it right back," Lambert added.

"Are you all right, Ma?" Ayden leaned over so he could examine her face.

She smiled and pushed him away. "It bruised my shoulder a little is all. But it made me yell, and Fletcher came out of the parlor. As soon as he saw the uniform, the man took off running."

"Why was the deputy in the parlor and not behind the door or someplace closer?" The question came from Mia.

Ayden glanced back to see her with her portfolio balanced in the crook of her arm and her hand sending a pencil flying across the page.

"More grist for your periodical mill?" Ayden's upper lip curled.

"Of course. People will want to read about this. Deputy?"

Lambert's face turned nearly as red as his hair. "I went into the parlor to warm my hands by the fire. It was cold in the hall."

"And quite understandable." Rosalie took one of his hands in hers and began to chafe it as though he were still cold.

Ayden cast his gaze heavenward, then turned his attention to the sheriff. "So should we move the child now?"

"For the sake of my family's safety," Pa said, "I would rather we did and let the world know so that no one tries to take him from here again."

"How will you all catch the kidnappers, then?" Rosalie asked.

"We'll find them." The sheriff's lips formed a hard, thin line. "That woman with the broken leg couldn't have gotten far from here. And I agree. I'll be taking the child with me, but I won't say where I'm taking him. Best for all. I haven't even informed his parents he's safe, so no one knows we know he was stol—"

Mia's gasp was nearly loud enough to be a cry. She stood with her notebook pressed to her side and her hand, still holding a pencil, pressed to her lips. Above her hand, her eyes had widened to near perfect roundness.

"What's wrong?" Ayden took a step toward her.

She flung out her hand as though to ward him off. "I sent some telegrams yesterday. I didn't think what I said was harmful, but . . ." She dropped her gaze, and her lower lip protruded ever so slightly.

"Mia." Ayden dropped his hands onto her shoulders. His insides felt like a clock spring wound too tightly, but he managed to keep his voice light, conversational despite an urge to shout. "To whom did you send those telegrams and what did you say?"

"I sent them to my editor and some other newspaper folk I know between here and the coast." She met his eyes. "I told my editor I rescued a child from the train, which everyone knows from our inquiries in town, and then asked the newspaper men if they knew of an abduct—"

"You sent that to journalists?" Ayden shoved his hands into his pockets. "Didn't you think how it would direct the kidnappers to us? Have you no decency but to spread his story all over the world?"

"How would the kidnappers get the telegrams?" Mia bent over her portfolio again. "If I don't, someone else will. I may as well get paid for it, as well as credit for rescuing him."

Ayden stared at her as though she were a stranger, as his heart compressed in his chest. "I don't know you anymore, Euphemia Roper." With a mumbled apology to the others, he strode past the sheriff and the now wakeful child, slamming the back door on his way out.

He should go to Charmaine's. He would find peace, calm, and polite dialogue there. She would welcome him without questions or accusations. Her smile would warm him, her beauty would please him, and her conversation would . . . bore him.

No, it wouldn't bore him. It just wouldn't hold his interest when he was as distraught as he felt at that moment. He couldn't even discuss with her why he was distraught. She wouldn't understand why whatever Mia Roper did made him want to beat his fists against something unyielding.

He lit a lantern in the stable and carried it to the woodshed instead. Nothing like an hour of chopping branches into kindling and splitting logs to renew a man's sanity.

After three-quarters of an hour, Pa entered the shed behind him and removed the ax from his hand. "That's enough wood to get us through

August, son. Now get inside before you catch a chill sweating out here in the cold."

"I can't go back." Ayden raised his arm to mop his brow. "If I see her with that portfolio, I just might toss it into the fire."

"Why?"

"Why?" Ayden faced his father, his eyes wide. "Pa, she has no sense of decency any longer. She's writing about the train wreck and all the suffering there."

"She wrote about how this town came together to help one another in true Christian charity."

"She's writing about how women are treated in their classes, likely looking for ways they are slighted—"

"She's writing about how much women are respected for their intelligence and ability to learn."

"And how all the professors are male."

"And how one of the professors takes his own time to tutor students at risk of failing."

"And now to make a spectacle of that unfortunate child and his family, giving them no peace—"

"You don't know that." Pa jabbed a finger into Ayden's chest. "You're making unfair assumptions about that lovely young woman, just like you did eighteen months ago, and you're not the only one who will be hurt over it this time." He cleared his throat and looked away. "You weren't the only one hurt last time. Your Ma and I love her like a daughter, and you took her away from us."

"I took her away from you?" Ayden pressed his arms across his chest. "I was the one who stayed to help you all."

"Is that why you stayed?" Pa propped a shoulder against the wood-shed doorway. "We haven't said anything to you about this. You're a man grown and have to make your own mistakes. But I was perfectly capable of continuing my work at the store by the time you chose to stay. That was a poor excuse at best. You were afraid to go east—"

"Of course I wasn't afraid to go east. I studied there for years. I was asked to return. I didn't apply."

"Then why didn't you go when Mia made it clear she would?"

The heat from his exertions dissipating, cold began to seep deep into Ayden's bones. Bone deep. Heart deep. Soul deep.

He yanked his coat from a peg and threw it around his shoulders. "It doesn't matter now. She chose to leave me, and I've chosen someone else."

Pa's shoulders slumped. "For the right reasons?"

"Of course." But Ayden couldn't meet his father's eyes.

Pa rested his hand on Ayden's shoulder. "If you are certain you are making the right choices, then your mother and I will accept them. Now come inside and get warmed up." He turned and left the shed.

Ayden followed, his footsteps dragging just a little. He didn't want to see Mia. He probably owed her an apology. He had made judgments about her work without reading it first.

Seeing a light shining beneath the sitting room door, he knocked and opened it. Mia sat before the fire, still in that pretty pink dress that looked vaguely familiar to him. She wore no shoes, only her white lisle stockings, and her hair hung down her back in a single braid, her pins lying in a neat pile on the table beside her.

She glanced up at him and hugged a sheaf of papers against her as though she thought he might steal them away. "Did you find the supper your mother left warming in the oven?"

"Not yet." He closed the door and approached the fire. As its warmth hit him, he began to shiver from the cold. "I can bring you more wood." He gave her a rueful smile. "I chopped enough."

"No need. I just wanted to finish making notes on this article, and then I'm off to bed. I have a lot of work to do tomorrow." She looked away and drew her stockinged toes beneath the hem of her dress. "Unless you won't take me to campus."

"I said I would."

"You've said a number of things you would do." She smacked the palm of her hand against her manuscript. "This is too long. I just can't identify what to leave out. I have heard so many stories and have seen so much during and since the wreck."

Ayden smiled. "I wish I had you for a student. Most don't have enough to say about anything. I give them a topic like the Wars of the Roses, and they say they didn't have enough to write a twenty-page paper."

They exchanged polite, stiff smiles.

Ayden crouched closer to the fire, absorbing more of its warmth. "Why don't you write a book about the wreck?"

"I don't think I have enough material for a book. Perhaps two or three articles."

"A novel?"

She laughed. "I am not Charlotte Brontë, as much as I wish I were."

"If you wish it, why don't you do it?"

Mia shrugged. "No time. I am always looking for the next story to write and sell."

"You seem to be doing well."

"I am for a lady journalist. But this salaried position will be less taxing."

"I expect so." Ayden shifted so he faced her. "I'm sorry about earlier."

"You were concerned about your family's safety with reason. I . . . well . . . I sent those telegrams, no matter how important the story. I didn't think the kidnappers would spy on the telegraph."

"Have you heard anything back?"

She shook her head. "I'm beginning to think they intercepted any return messages."

"It was a foolish thing to do, you know."

"Why? They hadn't come here before today, and we've talked about the boy all over town."

"The house was full of people until this afternoon, making it much harder to manage another abduction."

"Leave it to a war historian to think of tactics," Mia muttered. She rubbed her eyes. "I just want this story so much. It's exclusive and—"

"Potentially dangerous." Ayden touched her cheek, her skin as smooth as fire-warmed silk. "Everything is all right now. The child's been moved and will go home on Friday because you helped him on the train."

"What else would I do? No one else seemed inclined to do any good beyond saving themselves."

Of course not, except for Mia with her kind and generous heart.

His conscience jabbed him like a foil without its button tip, and he flicked his gaze to her papers. "I'm also sorry about the things I've been thinking and saying about your work. I shouldn't have criticized your work without reading it."

"Thank you for that. I try not to be a vulture feeding off others' pain. I want this article about the college to encourage other young women to get an education. Even if they get married instead of having a career, an education is always a good thing. What if they end up moving to the frontier? They can educate their children well and even educate the children of others as well." Her eyes sparkled like polished jade. "One thing I've learned while here talking to the women who graduated with me, and even before me, is that an education is never wasted."

"No, it's not."

It was what he'd tried to tell her a year and a half earlier when she accused him of wanting her to throw away her education for a life with no future. Her future was to have been with him, his helpmeet, his wife, the mother to his children, an intellectual equal who could keep his thinking clear and his mental faculties sharpened, no matter what he did.

And what she wanted to do didn't matter because it was all for him.

What a selfish, thoughtless man he'd been. Eighteen months earlier, he had cast a die he had weighted to land in his favor because he wanted to stay.

Feeling as though someone had stacked upon his shoulders all the wood he'd chopped, he rose. "I'd like to read your article about the college, if you'll let me."

"Of course." She smiled at him, not quite the heart-melting smile that tilted up the corners of her eyes but not the frosty, polite one she'd been giving him all week. "I only say nice things about the youngest history professor."

"Will you still say nice things after our fencing match tomorrow?"

"Only if I win." The smile warmed a degree or two.

"We'll leave here at eight o'clock, then." He reached out his hand. They shook on the bargain, and he left the room looking forward to fencing with Mia on Thursday morning far more than making an offer of marriage to Charmaine on Friday.

Chapter Thirteen

"*On guard. Prêt. Allez.*" One of Ayden's male students gave the call. Mia and Ayden saluted one another with their blades, then engaged. Ayden's right foot came down heel to toe, and his blade shot forward in a lunge, as Mia knew it would. Smiling, she feinted, then raised her blade in *quarte*, as though she intended to protect the upper left part of her torso. A second before the foil of his blade touched hers, she countered, circling her rapier to the right and down.

"Nice *octave*." Ayden smiled back. "A pity you're too slow." His blade tip caught the forte of Mia's blade near the hilt, knocking her rapier out of position.

She disengaged and retreated, then lunged fast enough to tap her buttoned tip on his chest. The student spectators gasped.

Mia laughed. "Too slow, am I?"

She attacked in *sixte*. Ayden was ready for her with his blade in quarte. The foils rang together. A *remise* of parries and repostes, lunges, and retreats began. Their blades flashed like silver lightning. The foil ends rang together like chimes. The forte ends near the hilt crashed like cymbals. It was a game of speed and endurance Mia doubted she could win. Her right arm ached. Her breath rasped in her throat, and she was forming a most unladylike dew on her brow.

"Ready to give up?" Ayden taunted.

"No." Even if she was.

"City's made you weak."

"Being a professor has made you boorish."

The students laughed. Ayden's gaze flicked their way for a second. Only a second. Enough time. Mia sent her blade singing down Ayden's in a *glissade*, caught her forte on his, and with an upward jerk of her arm, sent his rapier spinning through the air.

The students applauded.

Ayden's empty right hand dropped to his side. His lips parted, then he shook his head. "I can't remember the last time anyone disarmed me."

"August 10, 1854." Mia smiled, though her heart constricted.

She had been happy then, certain the world was hers to conquer and own with Ayden at her side.

"You might be right." He retrieved his blade and glared at his students. "Not a word out of any of you."

"No, sir," they chorused like reciting children in a grammar school.

Then they dispersed, snickering behind their hands.

"I'm undone." Ayden grinned. "That little move of yours will be all over the campus before I get to class."

"You should have remembered it. I remembered all yours." She switched her borrowed rapier to her left hand and held out her right. "It was only because I have fenced with you so often I got anywhere near under your guard."

Ayden took her hand, shook it, and kept holding it. "You've gotten under my guard, all right."

The way he held her gaze along with her hand told Mia he meant far more than her trick with the blade. In a moment, he would have gotten under her guard, and she would be undone to her soul.

She drew her hand free. "I have interviews to conduct, and you have a class to attend. But thank you for the match. I haven't fenced in about six months, not since that article I wrote about a ladies' fencing group. They made me have a bout with one of their champions before they would agree to be interviewed."

"Did you win?"

"I got the story."

"And an invitation to join?"

Mia snorted. "I said lady fencers. I am not considered much of a lady. I earn my living."

"Euphemia Roper, you could scrub floors for a living and still be a lady." Abruptly Ayden turned away and snatched up his coat. "I'd better get these blades locked up and get to class." He kept his back to her. "And since you humiliated me in front of my students, I think you should pay me back by returning here and helping Miss Judd with her essay."

In truth, she should interview the students, then leave the campus. She wouldn't see him the rest of the day. The next time she was likely to see him, he would be engaged to Charmaine Finney—a decision made to, once again, choose his career over her.

As she had done to him.

"What time?" she asked.

He told her. She sought for an excuse to say no. Nothing truthful came to mind.

"All right." She gathered up her coat and headed upstairs to meet the students.

Two young women had turned into four ladies and a half dozen young men, two of whom she had met through Genevieve earlier, one of whom had been her partner in their ill-fated sledding race.

Time sped by as she took notes, asked questions, and answered even more. They carried her off to eat lunch with them, and when she returned to the lobby, Ayden stood in the middle of the room, talking to Mr. Divine and Miss Judd.

He waved to Mia. "Just in time. Gerrett and I are going to help Miss Judd by giving her a match. Unless you'll allow me to get my revenge." He grinned. His blue eyes sparkled.

And Mia's heart broke free of its protective shell and tumbled at his feet.

Her feet half-frozen from tramping through slush, her cheeks stiff from the dried tears on her face, Mia trudged up to the Goswell house. If she was fortunate, Mrs. Goswell would be somewhere other than the kitchen—like shopping—and she could avoid her. She could avoid everyone until the trains started running, and she could escape from Hillsdale and all its memories, both old and new.

Instinct had warned her to run the moment she realized she was still desperately in love with Ayden. Instead, she had stayed, helped Miss Judd with her understanding of the art of fencing, and been far more honest with her than their short acquaintance allowed.

Mia pushed open the kitchen door and found Mrs. Goswell applying strawberry jam in the shape of a heart to the center of a cake.

"Fresh strawberries would be much nicer, but none of the hothouse variety got through this year with the trains not running."

"It's very pretty just the same." Mia spoke the truth without enthusiasm. "Is that for Rosalie and Deputy Lambert? Or is it for you and Mr. Goswell?"

Mrs. Goswell laughed. "It's for everyone. It's a spice cake, and I prefer brown sugar icing with it, but that doesn't look as pretty with the white sugar icing with the red."

"It smells wonderful." Which was true. The medley of nutmeg and cinnamon blending with a roast in the oven tantalized even Mia's knotted stomach.

"Let's hope it tastes as wonderful as it smells." Mrs. Goswell set down her knife. "Now, did you have anything to—dear me, what's wrong?"

"Wrong?" Mia kept her face averted. "I'm tired and cold."

"I'm sure that's true, but you have also been crying. Why?"

Mia compressed her lips in an effort to keep them from quivering. Her eyes filled, and she squeezed them shut to stop tears from spilling out. Instead, the action sent them sliding down her cheeks atop their dried companions.

She dashed them away with her gloves. "Excuse me." She tried to glide past Ayden's mother.

Mrs. Goswell blocked her way. "I was the closest thing to a mother you had for six years. I fed you into looking like a female instead of a beanpole. I taught you how to cook and dress right and talk like a lady. I even told my son letting you go was the stupidest thing he ever did. I think that gives me the right to know why you are so unhappy."

"A week ago, I would have told you that nothing I do is any of your business. But that was before I was back here and remembered that people here care about me." Mia dropped onto a kitchen chair and laid her head onto her folded arms. "I disarmed him this morning in front of his students."

"You're crying about that?" Mrs. Goswell laughed. "It's about time someone got the best of him. You'll be a legend here."

"I tried to help one of his female students with an assignment."

"Miss Short or Miss Judd?"

"Miss Judd. She gives up too easily, and I told her she was a coward who wouldn't even fight for love."

"Hmm." Mrs. Goswell drew out the other chair and sat. "Do you have reason to know this?"

Mia lifted her head. "It's embarrassingly obvious she's in love with Mr. Divine."

"I noticed that at church on Sunday. But why did that make you cry?"

"I told her she was just like Ayden, afraid to fight even for love."

A gleam brightened Mrs. Goswell's light-blue eyes. "Did he hear you?"

"I'm certain he did." Mia dug in her pocket for a handkerchief and wiped her eyes. "But I was wrong. At least, I was the pot calling the kettle black. I was the one who wasn't willing to fight for my love. And I still love him, and now it's too late." The last emerged as a wail, one like she hadn't uttered in front of another person since she was a child, if she had ever done it then.

And Mrs. Goswell just smiled. "It's about time you admitted it."

"It doesn't matter if I am. He's going to marry Charmaine Finney so he can stay here forever."

"Has he offered for her yet?"

"No, but he will because if he doesn't, his position at the college will end with the quarter."

"As if my brilliant son couldn't get work elsewhere."

"He doesn't want to go elsewhere. He wants to stay where people love him and respect him and he can do things professors aren't supposed to do, like muck out stalls and chop wood." Mia wrinkled her nose. "And my work is in Boston. Nothing has changed in a year and a half."

"Apparently not." Mrs. Goswell stood and resumed decorating the cake. "You prefer your career to love and community, and he prefers his career to love and true companionship. And have either of you ever wondered if your roads are the best ones for you?"

Mia curled her fingers around the edge of the table and gnawed on the inside of her lower lip. Finally, she shook her head. "I thought it was. I mean, of course this is the right road. Everything fell into place for me in Boston."

"Except that position didn't last, did it? And now you worry every day about getting the next sale or if you will starve for lack of work."

"I can always find work, and if this all works out, I will have a permanent position again."

"Nothing earthly is permanent, my dear. And even if you found work until your old age, do your pencils and portfolio keep you warm on winter nights?"

Mia shivered, remembering how many nights in her boardinghouse she had longed for warm, strong arms to hold her.

But Mrs. Goswell lifted her knife and gazed at Mia, her lips curved into a shrewd half smile.

"You don't have much time to get him back, you know."

"I don't want him back. Losing him hurt too much."

"Getting him back won't be easy." Mrs. Goswell spoke as though Mia had not. "You have to make up your mind now. Tonight."

Mia rose. "Considering how to get Ayden back is useless if he is determined to marry Charmaine to ensure his future position at the college."

"Mia, I will do what I can to help, and the rest is up to you and Ayden and the Lord." Mrs. Goswell squeezed Mia's hand. "Now go put on that pretty blue dress you wore to church, and my husband will take you up to the social."

"No, thank you. I'd rather stay here and finish my articles."

"All right, then. Put on that pretty blue dress for supper. Everyone will be here. And that means Ayden."

She couldn't avoid dinner with the family. That would be unforgivably rude after Mrs. Goswell went through so much trouble. She would wear the one formal dress she had brought with her and perhaps wear her hair in a less severe style. Somehow, she would get through an evening with Ayden across the table from her. Meanwhile, she would lose herself in her work and not think about Ayden. It had gotten her through those first months alone in the city. It would get her through more painful months ahead . . . and the rest of her life.

She washed her face, accepted a cup of coffee from Mrs. Goswell, and escaped into the sitting room. Her manuscript lay undisturbed beneath the stack of books she'd set atop it, and she began to rewrite the entire article, rephrasing and moving one paragraph to another page, removing a few lines and adding others. By the time Mrs. Goswell knocked on the door to remind her to get herself ready for dinner, the article about women at college was finished, and she had begun the story of the abducted little boy ending up on one of the wrecked trains. If anything would make her famous, this article would. Even when the story became public and other journalists wrote about it, none of them possessed the inside information she did as the reporter who had carried him from the train.

If only she knew where the sheriff had taken him. With the boy spirited away, she didn't know how to end the story except, presumably, Jamie would be returned to his family once the trains were running again or the snow melted enough to clear the roads. She must figure out the answer to the boy's rescue, but not tonight.

Back and fingers stiff from working too long without replenishing the fire, Mia tucked her partially written manuscript beneath the stack of books and climbed to the room she shared with Rosalie.

"There you are." Rosalie grasped Mia's hands and all but dragged her to the dressing table. "Sit. I will do your hair."

Mia balked. "Don't you want to take the time to make yourself prettier?"

"I can do my own hair in a trice. Now, sit." She pushed on Mia's shoulders.

Mia sat. The woman who faced her in the mirror looked pale and tired with shadows beneath and puffiness around her eyes. "It'll take more than a new hairstyle to make me look better."

"Oh, that's right. Ma sent this up." Rosalie darted across the room, dipped a folded cloth in the ewer, then sprinkled a few drops of oil onto it. The scent of lavender swirled through the room. "Hold this to your eyes."

Mia took the cloth and laid it across her eyelids. For a second it burned, then the soothing essence started its magic, and the tension began to drain from her neck and shoulders. Rosalie's ministrations with the hairbrush added their effects to her well-being. So did the silence in the room, emphasized by the murmur of Mrs. Herring's soft voice reading to the children. For once, Rosalie chose not to speak but to work, brushing, twisting, and pinning with deft fingers.

Silence and a quarter hour in which Mia could do nothing but think. The former she rarely did beyond what was necessary for her work. Thinking too often meant remembering her childhood, with her father leaving and never returning, a succession of relatives who didn't want another mouth to feed, the aunt who didn't bother to feed her but made her fend for herself. She had been so lonely, feasting on knowledge. Then Ayden came along and introduced her to a world of family members who cared about and for one another and friendships that lasted over years and miles.

How had she ever left it all behind?

Because leaving was easier than being left. Because she had known Ayden hadn't been entirely happy in the years he spent traveling between Boston and Hillsdale to complete his education, writing to her daily, pouring out his heart and loneliness. He was happy in Michigan with his family and friends and the students he cared about so much.

Students he would no longer have if he turned down Charmaine Finney as a bride.

She could not take all that away from him, even if he did want her back.

She started to remove the cloth from her eyes.

Rosalie laid a staying hand over Mia's. "Don't look. Trust me. You'll be beautiful when I'm done."

Mia smiled and kept her eyes closed. If the cold water and lavender reduced the redness of her eyes before anyone else saw her, the stillness was worth the trouble.

She couldn't stay there and watch Ayden marry another woman. She had nowhere to live except for Boston, since she had no work in Hillsdale and not enough in savings to see her through to some sort of employment unless she did sell the story of Jamie's abduction. In the East, she had a permanent, steady position. And she would not have to watch Ayden squiring Charmaine to social events, to church, down the lanes Mia and he used to tread.

No, she could not stay.

Rosalie gave out a low cry of delight. "This is stunning, if I may say so myself. But don't look. We'll get you dressed first."

In another quarter hour, Rosalie allowed Mia to look in the dressing table mirror. A stranger looked back at her, a lady who had taken time and care with her appearance from the crown of curls atop her head to the pearl drops suspended from her earlobes to the flowered blue silk dress with its tiers billowing over wide hoops and topped with a jacket in the same color, forming yet one more tier to the skirt.

"This is too formal for a dinner with the family," Mia said.

"No, it's not." Rosalie began attending to her own dark curls. "Trust me."

Mia narrowed her eyes. "You keep saying that. It's making me think I shouldn't trust you. Do you have something up your sleeve?"

Rosalie giggled. "Not me. I never—"

She broke off at the sound of the doorbell. "That'll be Fletcher, and here I am not dressed yet. Will you go down and entertain him until I'm ready?"

"Of course." She might be able to finagle some information about the baby out of the deputy.

But when she got downstairs, she found Mr. Goswell and Mr. Divine with Fletcher Lambert. Ayden was likely still with Charmaine, perhaps proposing to her on Valentine's Day after all.

Mia felt sick. If the trains had been running, she would have gotten on the next one out of town, even if it were going west.

But she couldn't leave town until the next day. The men rose at her entrance, and Mr. Divine came forward to take her hand in both of his. "I'm glad to see you looking better, Miss Roper. Did you have a productive afternoon?"

"I did, thank you. Is Miss Judd all right? She seemed so distraught."

"I expect she will be quite all right." Mr. Divine's smile grew warm enough to embarrass Mia. "She's a resilient lady. Would you like to join us?"

"I should help Mrs. Goswell."

"Ayden was helping her," Mr. Goswell said. "Now he's in the sitting room reading your articles. They were lying out, so I thought you might not mind."

"I said he could read the ones on the college women and the wreck. They're—" Mia halted and compressed her lips.

She hadn't said he could read the one on Jamie's abduction. He hadn't liked the idea of her writing it, and she had left it on the secretary along with the others. She needed to retrieve it before it was too late.

"Will you all excuse me?" She spun on one heel, sending her hoops rocking, and raced from the room.

She nearly ran into Mrs. Goswell, who was coming out of the sitting room, her lips closed but curved up at the corners, as though she were up to mischief.

The smile broadened when she saw Mia. "Just in time. Go on in."

"Just in time for what?"

Mrs. Goswell didn't answer. She simply opened the sitting room door without turning around, then retreated to the kitchen.

Mia stood on the threshold with parted lips and widening eyes. She ran her hand across her brow, then lowered it to the same scene, an intimate romantic scene. A small table had been covered in a white linen cloth and set for two, with the crystal candlesticks in the middle holding long white tapers. Beyond the table, Ayden stood at the tall desk, her papers spread out before him, his shoulders stiff enough to balance the flickering candles instead of the table.

"Shut the door. You're letting in the cold air." That melodious voice that usually caressed her ears with its warmth sounded more like the air from outside that frosted the windows than the unheated air from the hall.

Mia shut the door. Her hoop stopped her from leaning against it, but she stood as erect as a schoolgirl about to receive a lecture for bad behavior and crossed her arms over her front. "You found it."

"It's not like you hid it." Ayden faced her, his blue eyes nearly black in the candlelight, his mouth grim. "Why do you need to write it?"

"It's money in the bank, and I need all of that I can get."

"Are you so poor?" His gaze swept her blue silk gown.

"I'm a good steward of my money."

"Just not others' privacy."

"It won't hurt anyone if I write that article."

"Won't it?" His palm slapped the papers. "It will further disrupt that child's life to have strangers swarm around him. It will endanger him further if others learn his family is wealthy enough to make kidnapping worth the risk. It will give others ideas of doing the same to other children."

"Don't be naïve, Ayden." Mia moved toward him with the intent of taking her partial article out of his reach. "People come up with ideas of crime on their own."

"Or do articles like this give them even more notions?"

"I write about incidents after they happen, after the criminals acted, not before."

"And if you didn't report on it, would so much of it continue? Don't you think as a lady you should stay with articles that uplift and encourage?"

Mia rocked back on her heels as though punched in the solar plexus. "How dare you tell me how to do my job. I don't tell you how to teach."

"Of course you may do your job as you see fit." He sighed and rolled his shoulders. "But you said you wouldn't write this."

"I said I would think about it." She waved her hand toward the table. "And right now, we need to think of how to get out of this cozy little dinner for two."

"I intend on handling it by eating it. I'm starving." He crossed to the table and drew out a chair. "We'll have less fuss if we just give in."

"What about Miss Finney? Won't she care that you're eating dinner with me?"

Ayden shrugged. "You're an old family friend now, nothing more."

Mia flinched. "You can dismiss your past commitment to me so easily?" Suddenly, she could scarcely breathe. She could scarcely see. "It meant so little to you?"

"It meant everything to me."

"Except for the part about you not coming with me." Mia closed the distance between them, the firmness of her strides sending her skirts swaying and swishing like wind-tossed treetops. "So what happens to your commitment to Miss Finney if her father can't persuade the others to hire you permanently? Do you abandon her, like you did me?"

"You abandoned me. You made a promise—"

"Don't you talk to me about promises. You made a promise to me." She jabbed her finger into the center of his chest. "You said you'd love me forever." She poked him again. "You said you would honor and respect my wish to write. You—"

He clasped her jabbing finger in his hand. "I had no future in Boston. You wouldn't listen to me about that. You wanted your own way without listening to my side of things. And now, Mia, mi amore . . ." He closed his eyes and raised her hand to his cheek.

The motion drew her forward. Her other hand grasped his shoulder for balance. He wrapped his free arm around her waist, and she was in his arms, her hands clinging to his shoulders, her lips clinging to his.

He kissed her like a starving man took nourishment—deeply, thoroughly, as though breath itself took second place to the cherished contact of the embrace.

Mia slid her fingers into the thick, soft waves of his hair and yearned for the kiss to never stop. But a closing door, a giggle, and the need to breathe intruded.

Ayden released Mia first. He yanked his hands from her waist and shoved them into his pockets, as though her cool silk had turned to hot coals. "I'm sorry. I had no right to do that."

She gave him a tentative smile. "I didn't stop you."

"But you should have." Ayden fisted his hand around his somewhat crumpled neck cloth. "I should have stopped it before it started. We have no right to behave that way." He began to pace from the table to door. "We're not engaged anymore. And we won't be again. Your future is in Boston and mine is here."

Mia clasped her hands at her throat to hide her racing pulse. "You would have to break things off with Miss Finney. And then—"

"I would have no future at all, which is a sorry reason to offer marriage to a lady." He swallowed. "I counted on this one so much and convinced myself so thoroughly that I adored Charmaine that now I have no job prospects elsewhere."

"And you are not willing to give up a loveless marriage and security for seeking teaching prospects elsewhere?"

Ayden turned on her, his palms up as though warding off a blow. "And when are you willing to give up your position in the East?"

Mia bit her lower lip.

Ayden smiled without humor. "I didn't think so. You aren't willing to go with me wherever I can find work because you might not be able to be a lady of letters wherever that is, or so you think."

"Or fear," Mia whispered.

"And I fear not being able to find work."

"So you'll still offer for Miss Finney, just to have a job?"

"And a wife who is a helpmeet, not a competitor to see which of us can succeed the fastest." He stalked from the room, and a moment later, the front door slammed.

The cry of protest she would not utter choking her, Mia snatched up her story of Jamie's kidnapping, tore it in half, and threw it in the fire.

Chapter Fourteen

*A*yden started walking. His footfalls crunched on the frozen snow, loud in the quiet of the night. By the light of moonlight and starlight and lamps glowing in people's houses reflecting off the whiteness, he paced through the streets, up the hill as far as the campus and beyond. His lungs ached from the cold. His heart ached from the love he had abandoned. His conscience ached from the actions he had taken.

Worse, his conscience ached from the action he had intended to make.

"What was I thinking?" Alone in the countryside, he cried aloud.

He was thinking that, with Mia out of his life for good, marrying a woman for whom he had respect and liking was good enough. Even without the benefit of being wed to the daughter of the director of his department, he would have made Charmaine an offer. He needed a wife and a home of his own. It was time to join the ranks of his sober and respectable colleagues where single men were always a problem in social gatherings. The hostesses needed to find an acceptable female to even out the numbers. Charmaine already belonged in those ranks, accepted by professor's wives as her father's hostess. So she was a logical choice for a wife.

But Mia owned Ayden's heart, and she was not gone forever. She still loved him. She hadn't said it, but her kiss told him she did.

But she didn't love him enough to stay. Ayden leaned against an oak and covered his face with his hands. Without gloves, his fingers were numb. If only his heart had remained as frozen as his extremities. "She will leave me with that story about the abducted child to make her fame and fortune. She loves her work more than she loves me."

But hadn't he loved his work more than her a year and a half earlier—and now? He had looked at the position in Boston and the one offered him in Hillsdale, and saw more of a future in his hometown with his family and friends around him, people who wouldn't expect him to behave in ways that countered his moral convictions. They had respected and been impressed enough with his academic acumen to want him to pass his knowledge on to others, but they had never understood the life he chose outside the college campus. At home, he got both, with the love of his parents and sister nearby, and his brother and his family frequently visiting home.

How could he give that up?

How could he not for the woman he loved?

Certain he would transform into one of Rosalie's snowmen if he didn't get moving, he turned his footsteps toward town. He didn't go home. He veered his course to a house too large for the number of inhabitants and pulled the cord for the doorbell with perhaps more vigor than necessary.

From beyond the oval glass pane in the door rumbled the murmur of voices rising and falling in polite dialogue.

Ayden rang the bell again.

The murmur of voices continued. Footfalls clicking on hardwood floors added a staccato beat to the rumble. Then Dr. Finney stood in the doorway.

"I need to see Charmaine." Ayden made his request before the older man could speak.

Finney scowled. "She is waiting on my guests. You are scheduled to attend her tomorrow."

"I need to see her tonight." Ayden's voice shook just a little.

Finney scanned him, from his head without a hat to his lack of an overcoat to his hands without gloves. His mouth thinned, but he stepped back so Ayden could pass him and enter the house.

Even the unheated entryway felt warm compared to the outside temperature.

"She's in the kitchen, preparing coffee for my guests." Finney's face softened. "Go get yourself warm." Already stooped shoulders slumping, head bowed, he returned to the parlor.

Feet dragging, Ayden rounded the graceful curve of the stairway and entered the kitchen. Charmaine stood at the table, arranging china cups on a silver tray. She glanced up at his entrance, and a cup slipped from her fingers.

Ayden dove forward and caught it before it hit the stone floor. "I'm sorry to startle you." He set the delicate china on its saucer. "I had to talk to you."

"I know." She sank onto one of the chairs and folded her arms atop the table. "I heard about your fencing bout this morning. I heard about the sledding accident yesterday. I saw how you kept looking toward the door this afternoon." Her face resembled that of a painted china doll—beautiful and devoid of emotion. But whether she looked blank because she loved him and the hurt ran too deep to show or because she simply didn't care enough, Ayden doubted he would ever know.

That made him sadder than if she had wept and wailed and clung to him.

He crouched down beside her. "I never should have courted you. I knew deep in my heart that I still loved her. I simply covered it up with ambition and my deep liking and respect for you. If she'd never come back . . ."

"We would have had a perfectly comfortable and boring life together."

"I don't think that at all. Believe me, Charmaine, you are—"

"Don't say it." She held up one hand, palm toward him. Her nose wrinkled. "I am a beautiful woman who will find someone who loves me one day because I'm intelligent and kind and worthy and all that rot." Her lower lip quivered ever so slightly, and the pale blue of her eyes brightened. "You know what, Ayden Goswell? I've heard that speech before."

Ayden rocked back on his heels, his eyes widening.

Charmaine emitted a ladylike bark of laughter. "You look shocked. Do you think you were the first man who's courted me with an eye to marriage? I am nearly twenty-five."

"Of course not, but I can't believe he let you go."

"You're letting me go."

"I discovered I still love another lady. Surely . . ." He rose to slide more wood into the stove.

"Surely he didn't leave me for the same reason? No, he loved me. His name was Dermott Druggett. He had eyes as blue as yours but hair the color of a raven. He was ten times richer than Daddy, but because he spoke with an Irish accent and grew up on the streets of Dublin, Daddy didn't approve. So when Daddy commanded me to leave Philadelphia, Dermott tried to convince me he didn't love me enough to wed me, just enough to let me go free."

Ayden slammed the lid on the wood box. "He was a fool not to simply drag you away."

"Or maybe I was the fool to listen to my father and let him go away."

Memories flashed through Ayden's mind. "I wondered why you always looked sad when Philadelphia and your time there came up."

"Yes, I was happy there, even before I met Dermott. I fit in more than I do with the ladies here." Charmaine rose and pulled the coffeepot from the stove. "Will Mia stay here?"

"She has a position back in Boston, and I am likely not going to have one here for long. But if she'll have me, I'll go and muck out stables until I find teaching work, if I must."

"I'm not supposed to tell you this, but you are going to be offered the permanent position at the college. They are going to notify the other candidates and you tomorrow."

Ayden's heart leaped, then raced until it stumbled and twisted, knowing what he was giving up. What he must give up. "I'll still go to her."

"I want to be loved like that." Charmaine blinked back tears.

Ayden took her hands in his. "I think you were. He let you go so you didn't have to choose between loyalty to your father and loyalty to him."

"Then I was the one who didn't love him enough to make the choice for him." She rose on tiptoe and kissed his cheek. "I wish Miss Roper would choose to stay here with you. This is a fine place to raise a family for people like you and Miss Roper. But I think perhaps it's time I went back to the city I love."

"To him?"

"If he'll have me."

"He will." He embraced her as a friend, a lady for whom he had more liking than he had throughout their courtship. Then he left the house. On his way home, he said a prayer for Charmaine to have the strength to go after the man she still loved, a man about whom she had told him nothing other than her regrets of having to leave the East, likely for the same reason Ayden had told her nothing of his feelings for Mia. They wanted the same things—security, family, a position of respect, and purpose in the community. Marriage to one another would have given them both that. They would have had everything but the people they truly loved.

A little light-headed over the enormous error they had both come too close to making in the name of ambition, Ayden slipped in through the back door of his house, into the kitchen, the only room where a light still burned.

His parents sat at the table, drinking tea and holding hands. Thirty-five years of marriage, and they still held hands across a table.

They glanced up at his entrance and smiled below raised eyebrows.

"You look cold," Ma observed. "Are you trying to catch a lung fever by going out without a hat or gloves or an overcoat?"

"I didn't think about the cold. I didn't think at all. I just had to get away."

"Why?" Pa's dark-blue eyes pinned Ayden to the center of the floor. "What did you say to her?"

"Or she to you?" Ma added.

Despite the chill still racing through him, Ayden's face heated, and he tried to look away. "It's not what either of us said. It's, um . . ." He shifted from foot to foot, like a child commanded to confess slipping a garter snake into Rosalie's bed, knowing the consequences would prove uncomfortable. "I kissed her."

"Then I presume you intend to marry her." Pa made a statement; he didn't ask a question.

Ayden nodded. "If she'll have me."

"Will you move to Boston?" Ma asked.

"At the end of this quarter, yes. Tomorrow morning, I'll withdraw my application for the permanent position."

"What will you do to support her in the city?" Pa asked.

Ayden smiled. "Euphemia Roper is perfectly capable of support-ing herself. And I'll find work. Maybe not teaching at first, but I'll find something. What I do doesn't matter if I'm with her. And . . .

and . . ." He faltered. "And she wants me there with her." He took a step back to the door. "Is she upstairs? I'd like to tell her . . . ask her . . ."

Pa shook his head. "Not tonight. I think, because of what you did to her in the past, you need to withdraw your application first and then make her an offer."

Ayden opened his mouth to protest but saw the wisdom of his father's counsel and inclined his head. "I'll be on campus first thing in the morning."

His parents' faces shone with pride and love as they wished him good night.

Certain he wouldn't sleep, Ayden went into the sitting room to write the letter withdrawing his application for the professorship at the college. A few embers glowed on the hearth. As he started to add kindling to replenish the flames, he noticed a scrap of paper singed on one edge but not consumed. He plucked it out and read what words showed on the torn bit of paper.

Ransom note fo

Two full words and a partial one were all Ayden needed to see to realize she had burned her story about the abducted child.

"It could just be a draft." He sprinted for the desk.

Her other two articles lay in neat stacks held down by books. Nowhere did he find a single word about the abduction.

"Oh, Mia, mi amore." He clung to the secretary like it was an anchor that kept him from sailing up the stairs and pounding on Rosalie's door.

His parents were right. He needed to sever his ties to Hillsdale completely before he could go to Mia offering her a heart unfettered to anything but hers.

He drew out paper, pen, and ink and began to write his letter of resignation.

Chapter Fifteen

In ten minutes, the first train in over a week was scheduled to pull into Hillsdale, the town Mia Roper hoped to call home once again. Whether or not she had calculated correctly and that home would be with Ayden Goswell, she didn't know. He had come home after she was in bed and left before she rose, without leaving her a message. Nonetheless, she bundled up in her warm clothes, tucked her handbag and portfolio under her arm, and headed for the train depot in town.

The station resembled a lemonade stand during a Fourth of July celebration. Lines snaked out the door and around the corner. Voices rose and fell in animated dialogue, and children wove through the crowd in a game of tag, their clear voices piercing the frosty air like bells. Even waiting in the cold, people smiled and chattered, their faces bright and hopeful.

"Those with eastbound tickets for today get on first," a railroad worker shouted from the depot doorway. "Tickets for today. Right now, we have no more seats on this incoming eastbound train."

Many faces fell. A few groans rose into the crystal sky.

"Westbound?" some shouted.

The conductor leaned back into the depot, then stepped outside again. "Westbound train has a few seats available. First come, first served."

"Ma, we'll never get there in time," an adolescent boy protested.

"I'm just believing the good Lord will provide," announced a woman with a baby in her arms.

A chorus of "Amen" swelled through the crowd.

Mia started past the line, headed for the station doorway. If she could get her money back for her ticket, she would have more than enough to support herself until she sold her articles and got paid for them.

Mrs. Goswell offered her a room in their house for as long as Mia wanted to stay. "We have the space now Mr. Divine and the Herrings are leaving us."

But if Ayden ended up offering Charmaine marriage after all, Mia didn't want to meet him over the breakfast table.

Heart pounding, she explained to the conductor at the door that she had a ticket to exchange and a telegram to send. He waved her inside to the ticket counter. A rotund man with white hair standing on end in the hot, dry air examined tickets and waved people through the door to the platform with the rapidity of a steam shuttle.

"Next," he barked to the shorter line before him. "People are waiting. Have your ticket ready."

Mia joined the line and drew forth her ticket. When her turn came, she laid it on the counter. "I would like to redeem this ticket. I am not returning to Boston at this time."

Without looking at her, the agent picked up the ticket, glanced at it, then handed it back to her. "You'll get more money for it if you sell it outside."

"But I—" Mia blinked.

More money meant she could leave the Goswells sooner rather than later—just in case . . .

She retrieved her ticket, then crossed to the telegraph office. Her message was brief.

NOT RETURNING STOP SENDING TWO
ARTICLES STOP

The secure future she craved from childhood sent flying with that telegram, Mia headed back out the door. More passengers filed into the station.

"Eastbound train is filled," the ticket agent shouted.

"When's the next train?" several people chorused.

"Eastbound tonight," the conductor answered. "Twelve hours."

The holiday mood subsided.

"There's a little lady here willing to sell hers." The ticket agent pointed at Mia, who was hovering in the doorway.

A sea of hopeful faces turned toward Mia. She clutched her handbag more closely, fearing that someone would snatch it with the precious ticket.

Gold and silver flashed before her eyes, along with shouts of offers to buy. She scanned the crowd to see who most needed the ticket. Her gaze fell on the woman with the infant.

She shook her head. "I only have the cost of the ticket, nothing extra. But don't worry about me. The Lord will provide."

The sums shoved in Mia's face tempted her. Those coins signified independence and security for weeks.

She ducked beneath the arm of a gentleman in a silk hat and walked up to the woman. "Take it, and God bless."

The woman's eyes glowed. "You're certain? You can get so much more from others."

"Keep your coin. Get you and your baby home."

"Thank you." The woman started to cry. "My husband hasn't seen our baby yet. Bless you. Thank you."

Mia gave her a nudge. "Get on that platform before the train arrives."

Her heart warm and calm for the first time in eighteen months, Mia watched the woman until she vanished into the station. Then she took a step back out of the throng and into something hard pressed to her spine.

"Say nothing, and no one'll get hurt," a male voice rasped in her ear.

A chill deeper than the cold air ran through Mia. "What do you want from me?"

"What do you think? The child."

Ayden's heart raced with anticipation, with apprehension, with exertion from his jog from campus to home in order to see Mia as quickly as possible. But when he reached the house, Rosalie was home alone.

"She left for the train station over an hour ago," Rosalie said.

"The train?" A lump swelled in Ayden's chest. "She left? I thought . . . I was certain . . ."

He had just destroyed his future for a lady who still found her career more important than he was.

Rosalie giggled and kissed his cheek. "Don't look so woebegone, brother. She didn't leave Hillsdale. She went there to turn in her ticket. Of course, I did expect her back sooner than this. Maybe she changed her mind."

"I'll change my mind about Lambert if you're not careful." Ayden tugged on one of Rosalie's curls, causing the left side of her coiffure to tumble onto her shoulder.

"Oh, you." She gave him a playful slap on his hand, but sobered at once. "Seriously, Ayden, she should have come home by now. She didn't take her things with her except for her notebook and purse, and if she was just going to turn in her—"

Her voice died behind him as he slammed out the kitchen door.

He reached the station in minutes and began searching the crowd for signs of Mia. He found lots of females, mothers, wives, and daughters trying to get passage on one of the trains finally able to get down the tracks to the east and west. There was no sign of Mia.

After a quarter hour, he managed to reach the ticket counter. "Did you see a pretty young woman come by here?" At the man's blank look, he clarified, "Chestnut hair. Green eyes. A hood with white fur."

"'Bout an hour ago." The ticket clerk tapped his chin. "She wanted to get a refund for her ticket. I suggested she sell it. Get more money."

Ayden's heart leaped. "Did she?"

"Nope. She gave it away."

She gave away her ticket. She was staying.

Ayden would have run through the streets singing about what a blessed man he was—if only he knew where Mia had gone.

"Did you see—"

"Look, mister, I have a hundred people to get out of here. I can't keep track of one foolish female."

"Of course not. Thank you for your help."

Ayden left the station. Perhaps she had gone to Genevieve's or to the boardinghouse or even to the church. She might have gone to the sheriff for information on the child.

But no, she had tossed that article into the fire.

Those who knew about her telegrams wouldn't know that. They might think she had visited the station to pass along or gather more information.

His guts coiling like a snake ready to spring, Ayden ran to Genevieve's house. Only the merest hint of smoke puffed from the kitchen chimney, and no one answered his knock. Likewise, the church, for the first time in a week, lay quiet and empty.

Footfalls slowing, Ayden made his way toward the sheriff's office. He saw a few acquaintances along the way and asked about Mia. No one had seen her. Mouth dry and temples beginning to throb, Ayden entered the sheriff's office.

For once, he was glad to see Fletcher Lambert on duty.

"How may I help you?" Lambert, now his future brother-in-law, grinned and raised a hand in greeting.

"Mia is missing." Ayden grasped the edge of the counter. "She went to the train station to turn in her ticket, and no one has seen her since."

"You're sure." Lambert leaned forward, his eyes growing dark. "She's not—"

"Anywhere unless she's gotten home in the last quarter hour or so."

"Let's go see." Lambert stepped into the back office for a moment, then returned, pulling on his overcoat. "Sheriff says I can go with you. All the others are guarding the station." He lowered his voice though the office was empty. "We sent the child home this morning, but the kidnappers are still at large and aren't likely to know we no longer have the boy here."

The child. The kidnappers. They would surely not bother with Mia. She knew nothing.

But she had sent those telegrams, and the kidnappers might think she did.

Ayden and Lambert sprinted for the Goswell house. Halfway there, they met Rosalie racing through the slush, waving a sheet of paper and screaming.

The gun pressing into her ribs prodding her forward in silence, Mia stumbled through the trees and into an overgrown but still familiar yard. She knew the yard, the back of the house, and the kitchen into which the false railroad worker shoved her.

Through her own blurred vision and a pall of smoke from a charcoal brazier in the middle of the stone floor, she peered at a table where she had often helped prepare lemonade and sweets to feed hungry college students, the stove where she had set many a pot of coffee to brew. The stove lay cold, and the table served as a bed for a woman with one leg splinted and swathed in bandages. Nothing else in the chamber stayed the same as the last time she had visited Professor and Mrs. Blamey. Black cloth covered the windows instead of frilly gingham. Candles flickered in holders atop the stove and the shelves meant for dishes. The only warmth radiated from the brazier, pitiful at best, little use in a frigid Michigan February.

Shivering uncontrollably, her mouth dry, Mia fixed her attention on the woman and tried to speak in a voice that gave away nothing of her desire to scream. "You've been holed up here all along? We intended to help you."

"I crawled out the back of the car the minute I realized you had the Yardley brat." The woman's voice was tight. Lines of pain etched her face. "If my leg weren't broke already, it were broke after I landed on the ground, you interfering—"

"Enough talking." The gunman closed the door and shoved Mia forward. "Where are the others?"

"Sleeping in the dining room." The woman closed her eyes and fumbled a flat green bottle to her lips. The stench of spirits and something else filled the room, along with the smoke. Laudanum. The woman must be in terrible pain.

Mia hugged her arms over her middle. "Help me, and we can get you proper medical care."

"Tabard here has done well enough." The woman closed her eyes. "Just give us the baby, and we can get all the money we need for all the doctors in the world."

"I don't know where he is." Mia doubted the woman would believe her any more than had her abductor. "I don't know. I don't know. I don't—" She heard the rising note in her voice and clamped her lips together.

Tabard nudged her with the gun. "Turn around. Agnes, tie her hands."

Shaking, Mia kept her hands tucked beneath her arms.

"Put your hands behind you." Tabard shoved the gun harder into Mia's ribs.

Mia put her hands behind her. "You won't . . . won't get anywhere like this. I don't know where Jamie is."

"Goswell does." Agnes began to wind rough hemp around Mia's wrists.

Her heart crawled into her throat, threatening to strangle her. "They won't sacrifice the baby for me. I won't l-let them."

Could she burn through her bonds with the brazier? She risked setting fire to her clothes and blistering her skin, but—

"We don't want to harm the baby. We just want money for him." Tabard handed his gun to Agnes and crouched to tie Mia's ankles. "But you are worth nothing, so we will harm you."

She opened her mouth to dispute his claim of no harm to the baby, but remained silent. If she didn't say anything, perhaps they wouldn't gag her.

"Keep holding her," Tabard said. "I'm fetching the others."

The others meant the other two men and more guns. They trooped into the kitchen and arranged themselves near doors and windows. Mia sat on the floor beneath the table and concentrated on not being sick. She must free herself, must warn the sheriff to warn whoever held the baby.

Black spots danced before her eyes. Her head filled with mush and muddled thoughts. Must. Get. Away. Must. Warn. Must—

The two men looking outside leaped back from the window and door. "They're here," Tabard announced. "I knew Goswell wouldn't risk the girl's life." He caressed the barrel of his gun, then turned the muzzle on Mia.

"You were the man on the railway car." A surge of energy pulsed through her, and she shot out her bound feet, striking him across the ankles.

Tabard swore and pulled the trigger.

Mia rolled beneath the table, kicking at the legs, a chair, the brazier. Agnes screamed. The men shouted. Another gun blast roared through the room.

The inside kitchen door burst open.

Through a tangle of hair and the rungs of a chair, Mia stared at Ayden Goswell, who had what appeared to be a child in his arms. "You think you can trade my lady for this child," Ayden shouted, "then take him." And he threw the child straight at Tabard.

Tabard dropped his weapon and grabbed for the baby. A second man charged for Ayden, gun raised. Mia kicked a chair into his path. He crashed to the floor, his bullet blasting away plaster from the ceiling.

Diving beneath the table, Ayden cleared the way for Lambert and two other deputies, guns drawn, to swarm into the kitchen and secure the kidnappers. Two of the men charged for the back door. Lambert brought one down with a shot to his leg. The other tripped over the limp body of the "child" and lost his weapon. Before he could retrieve it, a deputy held him at the muzzle of his weapon.

Tabard remained motionless, his mouth open, his eyes wide as he stared at the baby head he held in his hands.

"It's a doll." Mia started to giggle. "It's one of Rosalie's dolls."

"My mother never throws anything away." Ayden slid out from beneath the table and drew Mia after him. "Let me get you untied."

He produced a knife no longer than an index finger but looking as old as ancient Rome and sliced through Mia's bonds. Then, while the deputies bundled the three criminals and Agnes out of the house, Ayden held Mia close, kissing her brow, her eyes, and, finally, her lips. "I love you, Mia, mi amore. I never stopped. I was a fool to think I could live without you even here. I won't again. I'll come to Boston or Philadelphia or Bombay, as long as—"

"Shh." She laid a finger over his lips. "No need. I sent a telegram to tell my editor I won't be coming back."

"Mia." He held her at arm's length, then released her shoulders to take her hand and draw her into the clean, crisp air of the overgrown garden. "Too smoky in there. I couldn't see your beautiful eyes. Did you say you aren't returning to Boston?"

"I'll have my things sent to me here."

"But what will you do for work?"

"I can write some articles from here and tutor and teach fencing and . . ." She gave him a coy smile. "Perhaps find a great deal more to occupy my time."

Ayden rubbed the back of his neck and took several quick breaths. "Like being my wife? We needn't stay here. I turned in my letter of resignation so I could go with you."

"Oh, Ayden." Mia lost a battle with tears and rested her head against his broad shoulder, weeping. "I don't want to go back to Boston. I want to stay here, where I am loved." She raised her head. "I never stopped loving you either. I didn't ask for this assignment, but an editor knew I lived here and asked me to write it." She toyed with the top button on his coat. "What about Charmaine?"

Ayden's smile was gentle, a little rueful. "Apparently she left for the East on the first train out of town this morning. She only left Philadelphia because her father would have stopped supporting her if she did not return home."

"She always looked sad when Philadelphia came into the conversation." Mia rubbed her cheek on Ayden's coat. "What will she do there if she has no money from Finney and no work?"

"She will do just fine. You see, there seems to be a certain Irish businessman out there she thinks is worth trying to remind he loved her once."

"Unless he's a fool, she'll succeed." Hand still shaking, Mia stroked Ayden's cheek. "But your professorship? If you resigned, how can you stay here?"

"I don't know what Charmaine said to her father, but Dr. Finney is"—Ayden shook his head—"subdued this morning. I thought he might cry when I resigned."

"He thinks the world of you. That's obvious."

"He said if I change my mind about accepting the position or if you were as brilliant as he thinks you are and decide to stay, I can reapply for the position. And if they decide against me . . ." He shrugged. "I can work with Pa in the hardware store or apply for work elsewhere—if you need to go elsewhere to work. I just want to be with you."

"Change your mind about accepting the position?" Mia took half a step back. "You mean they were going to offer you the professorship after all?"

Ayden inclined his head. "Charmaine told me last night. I wanted to make you an offer of marriage last night, but I needed to be sure you knew I was free first." He curved his hands around her cheeks and tilted her face up. "I needed you to know that's how serious I am this time about how much I love you and want you to marry me." He glanced around him at the garden where he had first proposed on a warm, moonlit night. He smiled. "Will you marry me, Miss Roper? I love you with all my heart."

"And I love you with all my heart." She rose on tiptoe and kissed him. "I'll marry you and stay here or go anywhere, as long as I am with you, Professor Goswell."

Epilogue

❉

Hillsdale, Michigan
August 1857

In ten more miles, Euphemia Roper Goswell would reach Hillsdale, Michigan, the town she swore she would never leave again. In ten more miles, she would see her husband of fourteen months and announce exactly why she would stop journeying to research her articles—both reasons why. That would make him happy during the school year when he could not leave his position as professor of classical studies at the college.

More restless than the children in the seat on the opposite side of the car from hers, Mia began to gather up her belongings. She wrapped the light shawl around her shoulders against the approaching coolness of an August evening. She hooked her umbrella over her arm and slung her satchel over one shoulder. Last, but definitely not least, she tucked her portfolio under one arm.

Ayden still didn't like her carrying the writing case with her every-where she went. This time, once she showed him the contents, she expected he would be happy she gave the worn leather such tender loving care.

And when he received the rest of her news, he would be the one providing the tender loving care.

She grinned at the prospect and gripped the back of the seat ahead of her, ready to stand and rush to the front of the car the instant the engine drew into the station. She wanted to be the first one onto the platform, knowing as she did that Ayden would be there to greet her after her two-week journey back East. She leaned forward as though she alone could compel the engineer to power on more steam and reach their destination faster.

The train slowed.

"Oh no." With memories of the wreck still fresh in her mind, Mia cried out in alarm.

Others merely grumbled at a delay in their journey. "Cows on the track or something."

"Or another train in the way."

"If we don't reach Chicago on time—"

Mia missed what would happen if the train got off schedule, as she rose to poke her head out the open window. "I don't see anything in the way."

Not that she could see from her car, which was near the rear of the train.

The train halted with a jolt that sent Mia tumbling onto her seat. Her portfolio and umbrella clattered to the floor. With some difficulty, she bent down to retrieve the objects, and when she straightened, Ayden stood in the aisle beside her.

She caught her breath. "What are you doing here?"

"What a way to greet the love of your life." He drew her from her seat and kissed her soundly, much to the delight or horror of the other passengers. "I have come to take you home."

"Did you think I wouldn't get off the train?"

"I didn't want you to get off the train at the station." Ayden released her long enough to bow to the gawping passengers. "My apologies, ladies and gentlemen, for this delay. Once this beautiful lady has come with me, you all will be on your way."

"But, Ayden—"

"No delaying these good people." Ayden caught hold of her hand and drew her down the aisle.

The passengers they passed scowled or smiled, and a few offered advice.

"That's right, lad. Keep her on a tight rein," an elderly gentleman with a silver-topped cane said.

"Don't let him push you around, young lady." The man's wife addressed Mia.

"Let one who looks like that one drag you anywhere he likes," another elderly lady said, then cackled like a hen with a newly laid egg.

Mia and Ayden laughed. Her face was hot with mortification at this attention. Ayden held his head high with pride.

At the door to the car, he leaped to the ground and held up his arms. "Jump. I'll catch you."

"You had better." She glanced down. If he dropped her, she would not land in soft snow this time.

But she knew he would catch her. His long, strong fingers curved around her waist, and he swung her to the gravel beside the track with a little "Oomph" of effort.

"This sojourn into the city didn't make you as skinny as a wormy string bean." He patted her hip. "I think you gained a pound or two."

"You aren't supposed to say things like that to your wife." Despite her admonition, Mia laughed and poked his ribs with her elbow. "Now what was that scene all about? I would have reached Hillsdale in a few more minutes, and if you want to be alone with me, we would be at our house faster."

"As much as I want to be alone with you, my beautiful bride, that will have to wait." Ayden led the way to the old chestnut gelding grazing a few feet from the track. "Your palfrey, my lady." He bowed, one hand to his chest, the other outstretched.

Mia stared at him. "Have you taken up drinking?"

"Only drunk at the sight of you, as always."

"Ayden, I can't ride a horse with all this stuff."

"I will carry your stuff and walk."

"But—"

"No arguments. Time is wasting." He divested her of umbrella, satchel, and portfolio. "Up you go."

He had positioned the horse near a conveniently fallen log. When she stepped onto this makeshift mounting block, Mia realized the horse wore a sidesaddle. One hand on the pummel, she glanced back to Ayden. "What is this about?"

He merely grinned at her, his dark-blue eyes glinting with amusement.

Uneasiness coiling through her middle, she mounted the horse, glad styles demanded abundant petticoats so her lack of a long riding habit did not matter so much and her modesty was preserved. Reins in hand, she snapped them, and the aging gelding shambled toward town.

"At this pace, we will reach town sometime after supper." She glanced at the setting sun toward which they rode, observing a trailing puff of smoke from the train engine and the distant outline of the town that had become the most precious place on earth to her. She sighed with contentment.

"How did I ever leave?"

"You wanted a career as a journalist." Ayden patted her knee. "And you probably would not have gotten the acclaim you have without having gone east."

"But I had to come back to truly see that acclaim occur." She gazed down at the man striding beside her, her heart so full she was certain she would burst with all she wanted to tell him when they were alone in their lovely home off Howell Street.

A year and a half earlier, her article about the train wreck that had sent her back into Ayden's proximity and consequently his arms, had been published in a lady's periodical, but other publications had gained permission to print her work. Donations poured in for victims of the train wreck and for the generous town that had housed them for over a week. Suddenly Mia found herself with more requests for articles than she could possibly manage, especially when planning a wedding, then becoming Ayden's wife. Too often, she found herself traveling for research, and when Ayden, hired by the college to be a full professor, could not go with her, it was lonely, not exciting, disruptive of the time she wished to spend with her family—Ayden's family, now hers—and friends.

But that was all done now.

Her lips curved into a secret smile.

"What's that look about?" Ayden poked her thigh through her layers of petticoats and gown.

She smacked his hand away. "No one may be around, but we are still in public. Save that kind of behavior for our house."

"Alas, I must, as we will soon not be alone at all."

Mia lifted her eyebrows in query, but then she caught a whiff of meat being cooked over open fires. Her nostrils flared, inhaling the succulent aroma of pork and beef nearly ready to eat—a great deal of pork and beef ready to eat. It mingled with the mournful wail of the train whistle as the train made the last curve of track before the station. Music rolled through the evening—happy, lively music that made a body want to tap one's toes.

She reined in. "What is happening in town?"

He shrugged and kept walking.

"Ayden." She nudged the gelding to resume and glared at her husband. "This is not Independence Day, so what gives?"

"You'll see." He tossed her portfolio into the air and caught it, distracting her long enough for them to round the curve into town, where a banner stretched across the street reading, "Welcome Home, Euphemia Goswell."

Beyond the banner, at least half the town lined up to greet her. The band played. The people cheered. Ayden took the reins from her hand and led her mount forward.

"It was not my idea," he shouted back to her.

Her friend Genevieve had organized the celebration, the welcome home for the town's most famous citizen.

"And the one who has done us the most good," the mayor intoned in his welcome speech. "We wish to honor you for the work you have done to help this town and victims of the train wreck." The speech threatened to keep going, but people began to move toward the acres of food provided by town ladies, like Ayden's mother and sister. They pressed a heaping plate on her, but she couldn't eat. She was too moved to realize that a woman like her—abandoned by her relatives, compelled to steal pencils and paper to be able to write—could be so honored by the town, so loved by its residents.

Especially one.

Ayden led her home as early as was polite. The door barely closed behind them before he drew her against him and kissed her breathless.

"Do not go away for so long again. Please." He tossed her hat onto a kitchen chair and her shawl over the back. "Promise."

"I promise." She raised her hands to his neck cloth and began to untie the knot.

He caught hold of her hands. "No arguments this time?"

"No arguments."

"But your writing. Your research."

"Is done for a while. The research anyway." She reached for her portfolio.

Ayden groaned. "Must you. I would rather—"

"Patience." She released the buckle fasteners and drew out a sheaf of papers. "I have a contract to write a book."

"Do you now?" With a shout, Ayden grabbed the papers and began to read. When he finished, he gave her a look of confusion. "I thought you were going to write more about the wreck."

"I am, but a novel instead."

"Oh, Mia, mi amore." He drew her to him again, crushing the papers. "My very own Charlotte Brontë."

Mia grimaced. "Not Charlotte. That is a little too close to Charmaine."

Ayden cupped her chin in his hands. "Still jealous of her?"

Charmaine had finally convinced the man she loved that her father would no longer stand in the way of their marriage. Yet Mia could not forget that Ayden had come within minutes of proposing to the other woman.

"Not jealous. Not now." Mia tugged his neck cloth from his shirt collar. "I still prefer to use my own name. Or perhaps simply Mrs. Goswell."

"I like the sound of that." Ayden's fingertips caressed the sides of her neck. "Mostly because a novel means you will have to stay home for a while to write it."

"And longer." She grasped his hands and lowered them to her waist. "By the time I finish with the book, I will be too fat to travel."

"Too fat?" His hands pressing on her loosely tied stays, Ayden gave her a blank look for a moment. Then his eyes widened, and his mouth opened as he gasped for air. "You . . . you're telling me that you . . . that we . . ."

"Yes." She flung her arms around his neck and buried her face against his broad chest. "We're going to have a baby in about five months."

And now her joy in knowing she was taking the right road for her life was complete.

ACKNOWLEDGMENTS

*M*any people helped in the concept and development of this story. Mostly, I wish to thank Patty Hall for telling me about the train wreck in my native state of Michigan. Thank you to Gina Welborn for the fencing match. And thank you to Kathy Davis and Melissa Endlich for initially seeing the merit in this story so that I actually wrote the whole novel. Most of all, thank you, my dear husband, for keeping my computer and my belief in love alive.

ABOUT THE AUTHOR

Laurie Alice Eakes lay in bed as a child telling herself stories and dreaming of becoming a published writer. She is now a bestselling, award-winning author with nearly two dozen books in print. *Romantic Times* writes: "Eakes has a charming way of making her novels come to life without being over the top."

Laurie Alice has a degree in English and French from Asbury University and a master's degree in fiction writing from Seton Hill University. She lives in Texas with her husband and sundry pets. She loves watching old movies with her husband in the winter and going for long walks along Galveston beaches in the summer. When she isn't writing, she's doing housework, which she considers time to work out plot points, and visiting museums as a recreational activity. For more information about Laurie Alice and her books, visit www.lauriealiceeakes.com.